Happiness Has a Slippery Tail

ABLA FARHOUD

Happiness Has a Slippery Tail

A novel

Translated by
Judith Weisz Woodsworth

University of Ottawa Press
2025

Les **Presses** de l'Université d'Ottawa
University of Ottawa **Press**

Les Presses de l'Université d'Ottawa / University of Ottawa Press (PUO-UOP) is North America's flagship bilingual university press, affiliated to one of Canada's top research universities. PUO-UOP enriches the intellectual and cultural discourse of our increasingly knowledge-based and globalized world with peer-reviewed, award-winning books.

www.Press.uOttawa.Ca

Library and Archives Canada Cataloguing in Publication

Title: Happiness has a slippery tail : a novel / Abla Farhoud ; translated by Judith Weisz
    Woodsworth.
Other titles: Bonheur a la queue glissante. English.
Names: Farhoud, Abla, 1945-2021, author. | Woodsworth, Judith, translator.
Description: Translation of: Le bonheur a la queue glissante. | In English, translated from the
    French.
Identifiers: Canadiana (print) 20250211610 | Canadiana (ebook) 20250214903 | ISBN
    9780776642598
    (softcover) | ISBN 9780776642604 (PDF) | ISBN 9780776642611 (EPUB)
Subjects: LCGFT: Novels.
Classification: LCC PS8561.A687 B6513 2025 | DDC C843/.54—dc23

Legal Deposit: Third Quarter 2025
Library and Archives Canada

Production Team

Copy editing	Valentina D'Aliesio
Proofreading	Tanina Drvar
Typesetting	Dany Lagueux
Cover design	Benoit Deneault

Cover Image

Charles Alexis Grenier, *L'Oiseau*, 24 in x 30 in, acrylic on Canvas, 2009.

 u Ottawa

PUO-UOP gratefully acknowledges the funding support of the University of Ottawa, the Government of Canada, the Canada Council for the Arts, the Ontario Arts Council and the Government of Ontario.

 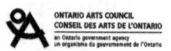 

Charles Alexis Grenier, *L'Oiseau*, 24 in x 30 in, acrylic on canvas, 2009.

L'Oiseau is an exploration of shapes and textures, which come to life through the use of sewing thread and masking tape, to create the image of a bird nestled in its birdhouse.

Grenier has been exploring painting on canvas and the art of collage for over twenty years. His style is based on a cubist approach, where geometric forms and deconstructed perspectives meet to create compositions that are both formal and poetic.

السّعادة ذيلها أملس

Happiness has a slippery tail.

Table of Contents

Foreword

When Abla Farhoud passed away on December 1, 2021, Quebec letters suffered a huge loss. Regarded as a central figure in what has been called *écriture migrante*, literature by and about immigrants, Farhoud was also hailed as a feminist who made women's voices come to life. Above all, she was a gifted writer who addressed universal topics such as love, loneliness, death, and dying. Mainstream Quebec media were quick to react to her passing, and praise for her was glowing. She was commended for her magnificent plays and novels, as well as her skill in imparting "lessons of humanity to her very last breath."[1]

Born in the Lebanese village of Ain Hircha in 1945, Farhoud immigrated to Canada with her family in 1951. She developed an interest in drama early on and became a television actress at the age of seventeen. In 1965, her family left Canada and moved back to Lebanon until the civil war drove them to emigrate and leave their homeland for a second time. Farhoud was with them in Lebanon for a short—and unhappy—time and then lived in France, where she studied theatre. She returned to Quebec in 1973. While completing a master's degree at the Université du Québec à Montréal, she wrote her first play, *Quand j'étais grande*, first produced in 1983. After writing several plays and short stories, she published her first novel, *Le bonheur a la queue glissante* (1998), translated here as *Happiness Has a Slippery Tail.* Further novels followed, all of them delving into the painful and inscrutable push and pull of immigration. Her last novel, *Havre-Saint-Pierre,* was published posthumously in 2022.[2] She was a finalist for numerous literary prizes and the recipient of the Prix Arletty for the play *Les filles du 5-10-15 ¢,* and the Prix Théâtre et Liberté, awarded by the Société des auteurs et compositeurs dramatiques de France, for *La possession du prince.* She is survived by her son Mathieu Farhoud-Dionne, a musician also known as Chafiik, and her daughter Alecka Farhoud-Dionne, a singer-songwriter with whom she wrote songs.

When her debut novel was published in 1998, it was hailed as both fresh and full of wisdom. One reviewer noted: "As Dounia opens the floodgates of her memory and reveals things that have been kept inside for so long, she captivates and moves us with the intensity of her emotions."[3] Critics commented on the author's ability to give a voice to so touching a character, a woman subjected to the misogyny of her own husband and, indeed, her entire culture. Her work had a far-reaching impact, as the following words suggest:

> It's hard to believe that her grandchildren don't understand her language. [Dounia] has learned to speak so little that you'd think she was mute. Yet, she moves her lips. You have to come closer to listen. Allow yourself to be drawn in by this faint voice that is like music, with sentences jostling each other, which her writerly daughter attempts to capture as she peppers her mother with questions.[4]

Farhoud was awarded the Prix France-Québec for this novel, which went on to have considerable success, not only at home in Quebec, but abroad as well. Applauded in France, it was subsequently translated into Italian, and has been widely studied in theses and scholarly articles.[5]

Many Quebec authors are well known in English Canada, and the English-speaking world in general, but Farhoud is not among them. Yet, her delicate and nuanced treatment of exile and immigration, alienation and identity, and mental health issues would surely resonate with readers across multiple communities, in Canada and beyond. There have been some translations of her work. Early on, a few of her plays were translated by Jill Mac Dougall, who also contributed an English translation of excerpts from *Le Bonheur a la queue glissante*.[6] However, among the novels she has penned, only one has been published in English so far: *Le sourire de la petite juive* (2011), translated as *Hutchison Street* (2018). It is very fitting, therefore, that this seminal novel be translated into English; there is also a case to be made for further translations of her work.

A distinguishing feature of this novel—and one of the most confounding challenges for a translator—is the narrator's use of proverbs, sayings, and other elliptical, somewhat enigmatic, gnomic expressions that she borrows from Arabic, her native tongue. The proverbs take various forms. Some rhyme in the original Arabic while others do not; some are expressed in classical Arabic while others are drawn from less formal, spoken language, some in the Lebanese variety of Arabic. Farhoud translated the proverbs, which are compiled in the Glossary, at the end of the volume. I have remained relatively faithful to the French version, although in some cases my translations have been adjusted slightly after consulting a specialist in Arabic translation. I have chosen to italicize the proverbs in the body of the novel so as to highlight them and distinguish them from the narrator's own thought process.

In the original French version of the Glossary, the subtitle of which is "Proverbs or sayings that appear in the novel or inspired the author," the last two pages list proverbs that do not appear in the novel. It is not clear what the author's intentions were in including them, but we do learn in the novel that Dounia's daughter, the writer Myriam, jots down these proverbs in French and collects them. Myriam, we presume, is the alter ego of Abla, who in real life may well have kept a collection of her mother's proverbs and sayings. The additional proverbs—the last thirteen—were likely part of such a collection and may have inspired her. The proverbs are listed in the order in which they appear in the novel.[7] However, those that are not explicitly used in the novel have been omitted from the English version of the Glossary.

Language is problematic and acts as a barrier to integration for Dounia, who speaks neither French nor English. There are frequent allusions to her silence and inability to speak. Yet, out of love for her grandchildren, she communicates with them in simple or broken French—all of which I have tried to replicate in the translation. Although they do not speak her language, the grandchildren do use the Arabic word *sitto*, instead of French terms for "grandma" such as *mamie* or *mémé*, which is a source of joy for Dounia. While the story unfolds in French in the original, and in English in the translation, Arabic remains a shadow language, present just below the surface. It occasionally makes its appearance in the form of the proverbs, which are not simply translated but also written in the original Arabic script in the Glossary, as well as in the form of names of people, places, and foods. These references have been maintained in the translation, except that the transcription into Latin script is generally done according to English-language conventions. For example, the name of the sultan "Rachid" is spelled as "Rashid."

There are other instances of heterolingualism in the text.[8] The family has emigrated to Quebec, where they settle in a francophone community. They are grateful for the kindness of the host society, personified by the Archambault family, who are regarded as guardian angels. I have attempted to preserve allusions to the French-speaking community and the family's attachment to their new home through the original spelling of French place names, such as Sainte-Thérèse, and by referring to Québécois characters as *Monsieur* or *Madame* Archambault, for example. In one instance, another character is said to repeat the expression, "*C'est donc de valeur, c'est bien de valeur.*" This is something that mystifies

Dounia, who never quite gets it. So, I have left the expression in French, keeping a bit of the mystery for some of the prospective English readers.

Dounia has grown up without knowing how to write her own name and is haunted by her lack of language. Later in life, her grandchildren teach her how to do so. Thereafter, whenever she holds a pencil in her hand, she forms the letters of her name, instead of drawing the birds she so loves to sketch. Quiet, reticent, "mute" Dounia lives in the shadow of her swashbuckling, voluble husband who snatches stories from her, for he can make them far more interesting—even to her—than she could have done. She nonetheless manages to tell her stories, from her youngest days to the end of her life. Her speech has been provided for her, her voice given to her by her ghostwriter daughter Myriam, who one day decides to write a book about her mother.[9]

Dounia is thus the Scheherazade of this story, embodying the age-old tradition of storytelling in the Arab world, captivating and inspiring the reader not only with her personal anecdotes, but also with fairy tales and moral stories that exemplify the rich cultural history of her homeland.

Although written some years ago, in the previous millennium in fact, *Happiness Has a Slippery Tail* remains timely and relevant. Dounia confronts very harsh realities, which she conveys to us unswervingly and poignantly: migration and displacement, aging and loss, conjugal violence and mental illness. Not without pursuing, and sometimes achieving, some degree of happiness, however fleeting.

Farhoud returns to these themes in seven subsequent works, all deeply autobiographical, including one that purports to be an actual autobiography, *Toutes celles que j'étais* (2015), which bears the designation *roman* (novel) on its cover, however, and which she admitted to having fictionalized somewhat. Each of her books examines, to varying degrees, the perspectives of men and women influenced by migration and their quest for identity in a new homeland. Her 2017 novel, *Au grand soleil cachez vos filles*, for example, returns to the subject of Lebanese immigrants who are drawn back to Lebanon after some years of living in Quebec. Mental illness, too, remains a leitmotif throughout her fiction, specifically addressed, along with the complex relations with other family members, in *Le fou d'Omar* and *Le dernier des snoreaux*. Farhoud's last novel, *Havre-Saint-Pierre*, finally tells the story of her father after a series of novels that began with her mother's story—a perfect bookend to her *œuvre*.

An important presence in Farhoud's body of work is the character of the writer. Writing is a continual search for understanding, as she says in the opening pages of *Hutchison Street*:

> My thirst for saying, telling, seeking, understanding, and finding has never been fully quenched. I feel like I'm always missing the point. And so, I begin another book, hoping to find the answer, but without knowing whether I'll recognize it when I see it, and, if I do, how I will put it into words.[10]

In *Hutchison Street*, there are actually two writers: the narrator who observes and writes about the inhabitants of her multiethnic neighbourhood, Montreal's Mile End, and a twelve-year-old Hasidic girl, who precociously makes sense of the world through the literature she reads—pointedly, the Quebec author Gabrielle Roy—as well as through her own writing.

Never afraid to go to a "dark" place, as her daughter Alecka has said, Farhoud made use of the art and craft of writing to convey her emotions. However bleak her outlook might seem at times, she was a "force of nature," remaining positive and marvelling at the beauty she saw in everything.[11] Abla Farhoud's legacy, in short, is to have illustrated the power of storytelling to bridge cultures, to shed light on the experience of the displaced, lonely, and voiceless, and to foster resilience among those in pursuit of belonging and a sense of home.

Judith Weisz Woodsworth
February 2025

Notes

1. Television anchor Claudine Bourbonnais, quoted by Mario Cloutier, "Abla Farhoud (1945–2021) : L'ultime voyage d'une humaniste en exil," *La Presse*, December 4, 2021.

2. See "Works by Abla Farhoud" at the end of this volume.

3. Lise Lachance, writing in *Le Soleil* in 1998; my translation.

4. Yves Paré, "L'enfance reste un sujet inépuisable et fascinant," review of *Le Bonheur a la queue glissante, Lettres québécoises* 95 (1999): 31–32; my translation.

5. An excellent example is a portion of the chapter entitled "Abla Farhoud: Montreal Migrations and the Ghost of Lebanon," in *Indigenous and Transcultural Narratives in Québec. Ways of Belonging* (London: Palgrave Macmillan, 2024) by Dublin-based scholar Dervila Cooke.

6. Abla Farhoud, "Dounia-A-World," selections from *Le Bonheur a la queue glissante*, trans. Jill Mac Dougall, in *Voices in the Desert: An Anthology of Arabic-Canadian Writers*, ed. Elizabeth Dahab (Toronto: Guernica Editions, 2002), 46–67.

7. In the original, one of the proverbs is out of order; the error has been corrected.

8. Literary scholar Rainier Grutman coined the term in *Des langues qui résonnent : l'hétérolinguisme au XIXe siècle québécois* (Montreal: Fides, 1997).

9. Cooke, "Abla Farhoud," 102.

10. Abla Farhoud, *Hutchison Street*, trans. Judith Weisz Woodsworth (Montreal: Linda Leith Publishing, 2018), 5.

11. Conversation with Alecka Farhoud-Dionne, February 5, 2025.

Acknowledgments

Not long after *Hutchison Street* was published, Abla Farhoud suggested that I translate *Le bonheur a la queue glissante*. She was particularly fond of this book, which she said was her bestselling one. I would like to express my deep appreciation to Lara Mainville, director of University of Ottawa Press, whose response to my proposal to translate Farhoud's first novel was overwhelmingly favourable, and to Acquisitions Editor Mireille Piché, who greeted the project with boundless enthusiasm. I am indebted to the production team, as well, for having expertly guided the manuscript through the ensuing stages of publication. I also acknowledge the generous funding provided by the Canada Council for the Arts. Abla's children, Mathieu and Alecka, have been supportive and cooperative in this venture. Alecka also welcomed me into her home for a fascinating conversation over a robust cup of coffee and greatly enriched my knowledge of her mother, of whom she was deeply proud. Huge thanks go out to Michelle Hartman, professor of Arabic literature at McGill University, who gave generously of her time to help me with references to Arabic culture, the proverbs, and the use of the Arabic language in the novel. The memory of my parents, who, like the Farhoud family, came to this country without money or language, has been an inspiration and a motivation for translating this account of exile and displacement. As ever, my family has been infinitely encouraging and helpful. I dedicate this piece of work to them, with much love and gratitude.

Happiness Has a Slippery Tail

I said to my children, "When I can no longer look after myself, when that day comes, you must put me in a nursing home."

They replied, "No, no, no. You are our mother, and we will take care of you."

As you grow old, resignation and wisdom are never far apart. And so, I said, "When a baby is born, you lay it in a crib and wait for it to grow up; when the elderly get too old, you put them in a home with rails around their beds and wait for them to die. Each country has its own customs, there's nothing wrong with that; the end result is the same. It's the cycle of life. I have lived the life I was meant to live, and I will die in peace without bothering anyone … *A self-sufficient peasant is an unsuspecting sultan.*"

The words that spilled out of my mouth were clear and orderly, with only the slightest hesitation that had become second nature to me over time. I had rarely uttered so many words at once, and I could feel the joy and excitement of a child eating an ice cream cone at the end of a long winter.

Even though my children kept on saying "no, no, no," each in their own way, in Arabic or in French, or by some other means, like Farid, who grumbled instead of talking, I could tell that they felt relieved. My husband Salim shook his head, rolled his eyes, and sighed, as he always does when he's irritated. He'd long since banished the word "home" from his vocabulary. When I saw him look over at me, I knew that he was annoyed with me for having opened the door to the idea. Myriam wasn't saying anything, but she was taking it all in as she usually does. Then Abdallah, my eldest, got up and declared vehemently, "Never, Mother. We'll never abandon you. You've taken care of us your entire life. I'll take care of you."

The room fell silent for a moment. Even my children's children turned around to look at their uncle.

Every single one of us knew that Abdallah could never take care of me. When the birds of prey came to peck away at the insides of his head, when he was disoriented and dispossessed, what could my gentle Abdallah do for me when he could no longer do anything for himself?

We were at the home of Samira, my eldest daughter. She'd invited us all to dinner, to be followed by a photo session. For once, no one was missing. It has never been easy to get all of us together for a few hours—there was always someone who was sick, or travelling, or busy. Samira, the chief organizer of the family, and Kaokab, my youngest child, had often tried to gather us together to pose for a family portrait, while their father and I were still alive. In the last, and only, photo that we had, Kaokab was a baby and Samira a little girl.

That day, it was the photographer who didn't show up, much to the chagrin of Samira, who even said that fate was against us. How can you speak about fate for something so trivial?

As I ate, I felt a bit sad. It was just a touch of sadness. Is that what made me mention the nursing home? I think old women should never be allowed to drink wine. I felt that something was coming to an end. I had the feeling it was the last time I'd be having a meal with all my loved ones gathered around me.

On the downslope of life, with or without wine, you often feel that something is coming to an end. One day, you can no longer climb stairs without losing your breath, and one day, you can't climb them at all. One day, you can no longer sit on the floor and then get up on your own. One day, you can no longer eat the hot peppers you love so much. One day, you can't eat anything at all without getting an upset stomach. One day, you have a tooth pulled, and then another, until you're left with a mouth you no longer recognize. One day, you have to wipe your mouth before kissing a child. One day, you look in the mirror and see an old woman who could have been your grandmother.

If my younger self returned one day, I would like to tell it what old age has done to me ...

Little pieces of yourself slip away, as noticeably as a low flame burning down. You can feel it, you can see it. Every time we try to take control of this strange body of ours, it keeps on changing and deteriorating until it's all over. We know that we're slowly mourning our dying selves, even before it's time for our children to mourn for us.

Old age is nevertheless gracious enough to come step by step, day by day. Otherwise, we wouldn't be able to accept it and tell ourselves that as long as we're alive, as long as our children and grandchildren are alive, nothing else matters. As our body ages, the value of things changes in our mind. And that's how it should be.

I looked at them, one after the other, but they didn't see me, fretting as they were about the photographer who wasn't going to come, and having quickly forgotten about the nursing home that awaited me.

My husband Salim sat at the head of the table. As usual, he talked and gesticulated, while I said nothing. I just listened. Samira bustled about, nimble and meticulous. Every one of her gestures meant something—everything had to be perfect. Every object in her house had its place; if it was moved, it had to be put back where it belonged. All the houses I've ever lived in have always been topsy turvy despite my best efforts to keep them neat. Samira's husband is as rich as she is, and they have no children. I, on the other hand, have six children and five grandchildren, which is all the wealth I have. Myriam, my second daughter, has two children, Véronique and David. She's the one I visit the most, because of the children. She writes books, but all I know how to write is my name. Kaokab, the youngest, is the only person I know who would win if she and her father were in a debating competition or a funny story contest. When she's around, Salim listens more than he talks, which is saying something. Kaokab is a language teacher, while I barely speak my own language, with just a smattering of French and English. Samir, the youngest of the boys, has three children: Amélie, Julien, and Gabriel. I don't know when he found the time to produce those kids—perhaps on an airplane, which is where he met his wife. One day he's in Hong Kong, another day he's in Brazil or in Chile. I don't even know where those countries are; I only know that they're far from here. Farid doesn't have any children and works at a thousand different things. He often designs and makes furniture, while I only know how to draw birds. And Abdallah, the eldest of my children, has neither a wife nor children.

I stared at them, one after the other, several times. I couldn't help wondering if they were actually my children or the neighbour's children, as they say.

A man I'd seen only once or twice before was sitting beside Kaokab. Next to Farid, there was a woman I'd never met before. Farid and Kaokab don't stay with the same person for very long. But if they're happy, that's what counts. My husband has a hard time dealing with that kind of thing. Although we've been living here for many years, he still finds the local customs outrageous. Especially when it comes to his daughters. Oh my God! When Myriam and her husband separated, he ranted and raved about Quebec, Canadian, and American society. It made no difference when I told him that people had also been getting divorced back in Lebanon, especially since the war, and that values had changed all over the world and not just here. But nothing doing. He was enraged instead of sorry. He ended up saying that the world was going to wrack and ruin and that nothing made sense anymore. His conversations always end on the same note, after which he goes to take a nap so that he can regain his composure or simply forget about it.

We were all very saddened to lose Myriam's husband. We loved him very much, even though he didn't speak our language. He'd been so good to Abdallah in his difficult moments. The only thing I said to Myriam was, "I think, my dear, that at this age children need their father." She replied, "Their father isn't dead; they'll live with him every other week." That left me heavyhearted. I could picture them carrying their little suitcases from their father's house to their mother's, with no place to call home. I just said,

"Are you sure that their father will be able to cook for them?" Her eyes were all puffy. She'd probably been crying a lot.

"Mother, all you care about is food. There's more to life than eating. But don't worry, their father is actually quite a good cook."

I thought, "You can't replace a mother." But I didn't say anything, I didn't want to make her any more unhappy. I'm not very good with words. I don't know how to speak. I leave the talking to Salim. I feed people.

My words are the sprigs of parsley that I rinse, trim, and chop, the peppers and zucchini that I hollow out and stuff, the potatoes that I peel, the vine leaves and cabbage leaves that I fill and roll.

I've been cooking meals every day for the past fifty years, and they're different every time. I improve upon my dishes. I make up new recipes and sometimes new cooking methods. I wonder whether there's as much variety in words. I use a spoon to stir food and only use my hands when I really want to. When I do touch the food that my children are going to eat, I do so with clean, bare hands. That's my way of treating them well. I can't do much else, but I know how to do that.

Salim and the children rarely say thank you. That's never bothered me. Do you say thank you when someone says, "I love you"? You can reply "I love you," but you don't say thanks.

Sometimes, I wish that I could speak, that I had a way with words. With time, I've forgotten a lot. Over the last ten years or so, I've occasionally tried to speak. Something will pop out of my mouth like a ball of wool that has come unravelled. I leave bits of words inside, and nobody understands me. Even to me, everything seems mixed up. I can tell that what's in my head has nothing to do with what's coming out of my mouth. When that happens, I keep quiet. The worst thing is trying to tell a story that I'm very familiar with, about something that's happened to me. When Salim is around, he takes over and tells the story over again from the beginning. He takes his time, pronounces each word deliberately, and gives a lot of details—even ones I've forgotten or ones I thought were unimportant. He gets up and waves his hands around for effect, to bring the tale to life. Everyone is enthralled, everyone listens to the story. Even me. All of a sudden, this little, insignificant anecdote of mine has become important. Even for me, the person who has lived through it. I don't know how he does it. I envy him. But I admire him, too.

And yet, I remember that I used to talk when I was little. I knew how to talk. Unlike my sister, who was always quiet, I spoke. I would say what I was thinking. I would make my brothers and sisters and my father laugh. Even our guests. Mahmoud Boutrabi was known throughout the village for his bad temper and foul moods, but then one day I made him laugh. No one had ever seen him smile, let alone laugh. My father took note of my feat, after which I became known to everyone as the person who had managed to make Mahmoud Boutrabi laugh. I also told people the truth about themselves, which made other people laugh. I didn't let anyone get away with anything. That's how it was then, and it was an easy thing to do.

What happened to make my words change into kernels of wheat and grains of rice, into vine leaves and cabbage leaves? To make my thoughts turn into olive oil and lemon juice? What happened? When did it start? It couldn't have been Salim's fault. If I allowed him to take my place, to take over my voice so quickly, it's because I'd already begun to do those things long before. But when?

The meal was probably very good. But I was eating without appetite. As ever, Samira complained that we were eating too quickly, that it wasn't worth cooking for hours just to watch her guests devour everything in five minutes. She was absolutely right, but what was the point of saying it over again when not a single word she uttered had ever changed this appalling habit?

Salim is always the one who replies when Samira makes this comment. He says that it's hereditary—that our ancestors used to eat from a large platter placed in the middle of the table and that everyone had to hurry and gulp down as much as they could to satisfy their hunger before the food ran out. He says that when he first arrived in this country, he never had enough time to finish his meal because customers would come into the store anytime they pleased, and since the children worked in his stores, they also ate quickly. He always ends his diatribe by saying that he eats quickly because he hates eating food when it's cold.

Old people always tell the same stories. I prefer not to say anything.

I don't know what prompted me to speak up. To tell my children to put me in a home, when I would rather die than go into one! Why would I talk about that now?

I have good children. They will take care of me. I'm sure of that, but can you ever be truly sure of anything? A single bad deed can sometimes make you forget all the good deeds that have come before. Human beings forget—that's why they are called human. Being ungrateful is not as unusual as you would think.

I would give my soul for the soul of my child, but the soul of my child is made of stone … Parents are devoted to their children and those children will act the same way toward their own children. That's the way things are.

Taking care of an old woman at home is very difficult. I know, because I cared for Salim's grandmother for two years, until she died.

Every person has their own life. My daughters have their jobs and my sons … Oh my God, why am I thinking about that now?

I worry about Abdallah most of all. Who will look after him when his father and I are no longer here? If my children are willing to send their mother to a home, will they leave their brother out on the street?

I'm sure that everything will work out. I'm healthy, thank God, I can still come and go and cook food. I take after my father who died at the age of ninety-five with almost all his teeth and all his wits about him. Why am I worrying prematurely? They say that *a tree can only feel the tenderness of its own bark* … With my six children and five grandchildren, I have eleven layers of bark.

Look who's coming! Nothing in the whole world is more beautiful than those three children laughing and chatting with each other as they walk along. May God shield them from the evil eye, may he protect them and keep them in good health … To think that just a few years ago, they were going to the daycare right across the street. I still remember how wonderful it was to spend hours watching them play. Véronique is growing so fast, and she will soon be as tall as her cousin Amélie. David looks more and more like his mother. Do I have some juice in the fridge? There are meat patties, nougat, and fruit.

They didn't stay long. I love seeing them, even for ten minutes, which is enough time to fill my soul with their image … And Salim wants us to move back to Lebanon, now that the war is over. He can go by himself, I'm staying here.

My husband is very different from me. When our children reached the age of six or seven, it was as if they became strangers to him. I can understand, in a way. He likes to tell stories, but is handicapped because he hasn't mastered the language of his audience. My grandchildren don't speak our language. They can say grandpa and grandma in Arabic, but that's about all. That doesn't bother me. We manage to understand one another and we get the basics, for which you don't need a lot of words.

It's relaxing to be with my grandchildren. I love them, they love me, and it's perfect.

Salim doesn't see life and doesn't live life the way I do. As he ages, he becomes more and more unhappy, while I'm just the opposite. Unhappiness has faded from my bosom. At times, especially when Abdallah falls to pieces as if struck by lightning, the pain comes back. But it blows over just as quickly.

When he left, David hugged me so hard it almost hurt. To think that just two years ago, I was stronger than he was. How he laughed when I used to beat him at arm wrestling or when I pushed him down the long hallway of their apartment. "You strong, *Sitto,* you stronger than Mommy," he would say. I wanted to tell him that I had grown up in the mountains, and that's why I was strong and healthy, but I couldn't find the words to put it that way, so I said, "Mommy, yours, sitting, always writing, so she not strong …" I understand everything my grandchildren tell me because they pronounce each word distinctly, as if they were speaking to someone who was deaf. If only the people on television spoke like that …

Véronique kissed my hand and placed it on her forehead. I was so surprised. That's what young people do in the villages to show respect for their elders. Where had she learned to do that? I hugged her tight, very tight, and took a few steps with her, singing, "Dance, dance, Véro!" From the time they were little, they've burst out laughing whenever we do this and, if I forget, they're the ones who chant, "Dance, dance, *Sitto.*" Then they wrap their arms around me and get me to dance. And the game hasn't changed a bit, even now that they're teenagers.

Amélie was in a good mood. She loves her cousins, and they love her. She didn't ask me for money today. Perhaps she was shy in front of her cousins.

I should call her parents to invite them for dinner; it's been a long time since I've seen Julien and Gabriel. I know what they'll say ... too busy, there's no time, send us the food by taxi. Well, no, I won't send anything by taxi. If they want to eat, they just have to come over. Too much work, too much work ... And in the meantime, the children are left to get by without their parents! I tried to tell them, but who listens to an old woman?

With Myriam, it's the complete opposite. It's not that she does everything I say. Far from it. But she makes me feel as if what I tell her is important. With her, I feel like the Queen Mother. All my children are a bit like that, but she is more so than the others.

Her children are like her. Grandma this, Grandma that, as if their grandma were made of gold or of chocolate and ice cream, which they love the most. Véronique even told her mother, "Grandma is a goddess ..." What a poor goddess I am! If all goddesses looked like me, there would be no reason to call them goddesses anymore.

Anyway ...

Sometimes, while I'm laughing and having a good time with my grandchildren, my children look at me and wonder if I'm the same person they had as a mother. And they're right. I'm not the person they once knew.

Anyway ...

I'm going to take advantage of the fact that there's no one at home and go have a little nap.

When I die ... I will miss my grandchildren ... and my children, too. I don't know whether they'll think of me from time to time. Silence is nice ... peace and quiet. I should have become a nun ... singing and praying and listening to the silence ... but I would not have had any grandchildren.

Some immigrants say, "I would like to die in the place where I was born." Not me. My home is not the home of my ancestors, or even the village of my childhood. My home is where my children are happy.

When my joints begin to ache, of course, I sometimes feel nostalgic for my teenage years. If I could go back in time, would I really do it? No. My home is where my children and grandchildren are. It's where I am today, short of breath, with my heavy limbs and my crinkly eyes that have grown smaller from crying and laughing.

My home is where my grandchildren are, clinging to my neck, calling me *Sitto* Dounia ... in my language.

I want to die where my children and my grandchildren live.

Myriam asked me to come spend the day at her place. She probably wants to talk to me about what happened the other day. I love going to her house, especially during the weeks when her children are there. I'm bringing them stuffed vine leaves and *hummus bi tahini*, which Véronique and David could eat 365 days a year without complaining. Myriam said,

"You could come empty-handed for a change."

"*Empty hands are dirty hands*, my dear."

"Oh, a new proverb, I've never heard that one before," Myriam said, picking up a piece of paper to jot it down in French.

I wanted to tell her that every proverb has its own time and place; it's used to support or refute what has just been said or done. This was the first time she mentioned what I had brought. Usually, she just takes the bags I'm carrying and puts the packages away in the fridge without even saying thank you, as if it were perfectly natural for me to bring her food. But I said nothing. I went to the fridge myself while she filed the proverb away with the others.

Myriam made me a nice cup of coffee along with my favourite snack—French cheese on toast. It's a change from the cheese I make myself, which I eat day in and day out.

I said to her, "Before I die, this is what I want to eat." She laughed. I love to hear her laugh.

My daughter Myriam doesn't talk much. She never has any stories to tell the way Kaokab, Samira, or Abdallah do. Even Samir when he has the time. Myriam doesn't gossip. When the family gets together, she is quiet, like I am. She almost looks like she's bored being with us.

When her children were little, she would at least talk about the funny little things they were doing, but now that they've grown up, that's over.

Even the Prophet Muhammad wouldn't be able to answer all the questions that Myriam asks me. The Prophet received his answers from Allah, while I am all alone ... And she looks at me as if she had never seen me before. Every word seems important. I can speak as long as I want, without worrying about getting things wrong. With her, it's as if my tongue were looser and my breathing easier. With other people, I'm always anxious to get to the point, and so are they. They're right, I don't know how to speak well. With Myriam, it feels like I'm a different person. At my age, it's annoying to be another person. I'm not used to it. Sometimes I tell her, "You say something for a change, I'm doing all the talking ..." She asks me other questions and, unwittingly, I keep on going.

I don't always understand everything about her. Maybe she doesn't understand me either. We both have the same mother tongue, but she studied another language for so many years and has lived almost her entire life over here.

Of all my children, she is the one who feels the farthest from me and, at the same time, the closest. I can't explain how you can feel so close and so far at the same time. If she didn't look like me physically, it would be hard to claim that she was my daughter. Even though I love her, and she loves me, I sometimes feel like I'm in the presence of a stranger: it's the way she hesitates, struggling to find her words in Arabic, which is interspersed with French words, and it's her way of thinking, especially, which is not at all like mine.

Like her, I hesitate and search for words, but it's different in my case, because I've lost something along the way, whereas Myriam has just taken another fork in the road.

I don't know if it's just a question of language or simply because she's from a different generation. Or perhaps it's her schooling. Studying for a long time changes a person. Even if we'd stayed in Lebanon and she'd studied Arabic, there would still have been a gap between us. When I went back to live in Lebanon, I noticed that those who go to school for a long time seem to nitpick. They use twenty words to say what could be said in three … *the best speech is a single word* … That's what I think.

The children came home to eat and then went back to school, making me promise to stay at their place until they returned. While she was eating, Véronique, the eldest, said to her mother, "I'd really like it if *Sitto* Dounia came to live with us." My children and grandchildren often talk about me as if I were not there. Véronique turned toward me to explain what she'd just said. I could've told her that I'd rather she missed me than get tired of seeing me too often, that her grandfather needs me, and that her uncle Abdallah comes to our house a lot and wouldn't be comfortable if he had to come to their house too often. But I smiled and just managed to spit out the words "me can't, you come my house, sometimes."

I told Myriam to go back to work, that I would do the dishes. She made a pretence of declining my offer, saying, "Rest, Mother, you have enough to do at home." And then she went back to her office.

I washed the dishes, tidied the house up a bit, folded a pile of laundry fresh from the dryer, mended whatever needed mending, and made some coffee. I placed the coffee pot, small coffee cups, and a glass of water on a tray, which I carried quietly into her office, as I always do when I visit her.

She smiled distractedly while continuing to type on her computer, as she always does. She took a gulp of coffee without taking her eyes off the screen, while I sipped my coffee and watched her.

Myriam doesn't let anyone come into her office while she's writing. Except me. I am so discreet that she forgets I'm even there. I never talk, and neither does she. Sometimes, she'll read and reread a sentence that she's just written, whispering to her screen.

Like me when I'm doing the dishes, tears sometimes stream down her cheeks. She doesn't wipe them away. She knows that the tears you shed take on the colour of your skin, and you needn't worry, no one notices them.

When she was little, she was the one who stayed by my side while I washed the dishes.

I love sitting in the rocking chair she put in her office just for me. I look out the window. The trees have turned all different colours. It's so pretty to look at. I'm drinking cardamom-flavoured coffee, just the way I like it. At home, Salim makes the coffee, but he doesn't like the taste of cardamom, and never puts any in.

I watch my daughter write. Her fingers are like flies trapped in a jar, whizzing around and always landing on the same place. Sometimes she glances at me without really seeing me … I watch her … My mother was about her age when she died. May God keep death away from this house.

I don't remember my mother's face anymore. I've been told that it was fair and round and beautiful, like the moon. They always tell an orphan that her mother was beautiful—it's the least they can do to ease her pain. Like me, my mother didn't know how to read. My father did. When the newspaper arrived in the village, at any hour of the day or night, he would read it from top to bottom. He read prayer books, too, because he was a priest.

Our house was an open house, as they say. I never saw it empty or just occupied by members of our family. There were always a lot of people there. It served as a rectory, a living room, a café, and sometimes even a courtroom. For those who travelled from another town, it was also a hotel and restaurant since the village didn't have anything like that. When my mother died, our house fell into complete disarray. My brother and I became so filthy that lice burrowed themselves in our scalps, causing infections. My father would hire many of the villagers to help him, but they never managed to do all the work that was needed.

And to think that my mother was supposed to have done it all on her own …

My father was distressed. As an Orthodox priest, he was only allowed to marry once, so he couldn't take another wife after my mother passed away. Since his eldest sons had already emigrated to Argentina, he decided to marry off my brother Musa, who was only seventeen years old at the time, to Nahila. Strong, intelligent, and hardworking, and slightly older than my brother, she seemed capable of taking over the management of our household. Musa didn't love Nahila, and this turned out to be the greatest misfortune of his life. For me and my little brother, it was just the opposite for we had acquired a new mother who gave us baths in lots of soapy water at least once a week … I've always loved water and soap.

I remember nothing about my mother except two sentences. If my grandmother hadn't repeated them to me from time to time, reminding me that they came from my mother, I would surely have forgotten them. She used to say, "*Never let moments of pleasure slip away; it takes very little to satisfy your body.*" I don't know if my mother had experienced a lot of pleasure in her life. I only know that my father loved her. Tears would well up in his eyes whenever he talked to us about our mother.

My mother also used to say, "There is no suffering that cannot be overcome by a good night's sleep." Despite the unknown illness that took my mother at such a young age, she never complained. She continued to work right up to the day she died. She wasn't free of pain until she went to sleep for the very last time …

The day my mother died, I didn't feel sorrow, but instead I remember experiencing great joy because of a small piece of lace I had wanted to have for a long time. Zarifi, a young neighbour who was a bit older than me, had given me the lace to make me feel better … to help me get over a loss for which there is no consolation, as I now know.

It's strange that I remember the name of my neighbour, whereas I remember only two short sentences spoken by a mother who'd showered me with so much love.

Myriam had stopped writing and was looking at me. I felt as if she were looking for something deep down inside me. She said, "I'd like to write a book about you, Mother." I laughed. Perhaps I blushed.

"Why me? Are you running out of stories? … Ask your father, he knows quite a few."

"I've written about fifteen books, and I've never talked about you. I feel like getting to know you better."

"What a strange way to get to know me!"

"Are you willing to do it?"

"Even if I said no, what difference would it make?"

I thought, "You will do whatever you want anyway. I've never read a word of what you've written, and even if you had written about me, I would never have known."

"How sorry you must be that you don't know how to read or write," Myriam said as if she'd been reading my mind.

"We only miss what we've once had, I've told you that a hundred times."

"You've told me, but I can't wrap my head around it."

And she began typing again, muttering to herself and angrily repeating her last sentence several times. Her fingers were more sprightly than usual.

In our culture, you don't tell your mother that she's lying, but I felt that she meant to say just that. I was tired. I couldn't wait for the children to come home. I walked around the house to stretch my legs and clear my head, but Myriam's words kept bouncing around in my head.

She doesn't get it because it's not true. Whenever my children ask me a question about my past, I reply with a saying, a proverb, or a stock phrase. It's easier to do than searching for the truth, telling it, and having to relive the experience …

Not knowing how to read or write has left a big hole in my life. But if I had admitted it, they would have asked me why I never learned, and then I would have had to start searching for the reason why.

It's so difficult to speak … to show how small you are … It's probably a lot easier to brag about your accomplishments than to admit to your children that you've let fate crush you, that you've never stood up for yourself …

A prisoner who knows how to read and write is not really in prison. That's what I've always thought. I've never said so because I didn't want my loved ones to feel sorry for me.

One day, I wanted to write to my father to ask him to come get me, me and my children.

I'd been in Canada for six months and was already five months pregnant. We were living at my mother-in-law's home, and my life was not my own. It was so different from everything I'd ever known.

Death … that was what death must be like.

They say it's hot in hell … But I was always cold, and I felt like I was suffocating. I don't understand how I could be cold and short of breath at the same time. Just before you die, you can shiver, your teeth can chatter, and you can have trouble catching your breath. I saw a lot of it in 1942, during the typhoid epidemic … I must have been dying then …

An iron hand was strangling me, and a heavy stone was pressing down on my chest. All day long. Without stop. I was awake much of the night, but I ended up falling asleep—thanks to God or my mother, who must have been watching over me.

I would have really loved to know how to write.

I couldn't talk to anyone. I didn't know the language of the country, I never left the house, I didn't have relatives or friends, and my husband had so many problems that it was impossible to talk to him. My mother-in-law—may God forgive her— hated me, so much so that it was as if I'd murdered her children.

My children were all I had left. The three older ones were in school while the two younger ones were still at home with me. It was mainly because of my children that I was afraid of dying. I had been an orphan, and I didn't want them to become orphans, too. I couldn't do much for them, but I could at least feed them and wash their clothes.

One day, my husband was writing. I knew that Salim was writing to my father—I could tell because of the way he would pause and think for a long time before starting to write again.

Salim loved my father. He respected and admired him more than any other man he'd ever known. Each time he got a chance, he would very proudly recount stories about my father's experiences, especially from the time when Christians and Druze were at each other's throats while the French and Turks quarrelled over their share of the harvest. He would tell the story of my father's adventures with such talent and passion that those who didn't know my father thought that he was an imam from the Prophet's time. Stories from that time, it's true, dealt with honour, justice, keeping one's word, courage, generosity, miracles, and so on.

Salim would write to my father regularly, and my father would answer him just as swiftly. When Salim read these letters to me, he seemed to be completely transformed. Sometimes, I had the impression that I was no longer my father's daughter, and that Salim had usurped my place. I thought, "If it makes him happy, why not ..." Salim had lost his own father when he was so young ...

Salim had just finished writing his letter, which he folded and stuffed into an envelope. Then he got up to go somewhere, I don't know where. I looked at the envelope for a few moments. I would have liked to turn into a particle of dust, or an insect, to be able to slip into that envelope and fly away, leave home, die … I opened the envelope and wrote at the bottom of the last page, as best I could, the few letters I knew how to write … At that time, I didn't know how to write my name yet. I was thirty years old, I had five children, with a sixth on the way, and I didn't even know how to write my name.

I quickly sealed the envelope back up before Salim could see me. He would have asked me what I was doing, and I wouldn't have known what to say to him.

For a long time, I waited for my father's reply. With every new letter, my heart almost burst from beating so hard.

I eventually forgot all about it.

Imagine if my father had understood some of my scribbling … I know now that was just wishful thinking, that I was just grasping at straws, *hanging on to the strings of the wind* … And even if he had figured out what my message meant, would he have taken the boat like I did with my children, and come to get us? Although always prepared to save the world, lift up the needy, attend to the wretched, and rescue widows and orphans, would he have saved his own daughter from death?

"It's your fate, my daughter. You made your bed, now lie in it." That's what he would have told me.

I was well aware that it was my fate. I didn't need anyone to tell me what I already knew, but I could have used someone to help me do what I was unable to do all alone. I would have needed an outstretched hand to extricate me from that cold, black hole.

Now, it's too late. When I really needed help, there was no one.

The letter that I so longed to write should have been sent to my mother. My mother would have understood, I'm certain of it.

It's impossible to write to dead people; it's impossible to write to the living. It's impossible to speak to the living, just as it's impossible to speak to the dead. I was all alone in a frigid desert. Even if I had been able to scream, there was no one to hear my cries, and no one to comfort me. I waited. For a long time. I breathed just enough so that I wouldn't die. So that my children would have a mother. I now know that the suffering of mothers who take their own lives is greater than the love they feel for their children. I was lucky. The love I had for my children was stronger than my pain. Perhaps I knew, even at that time, that everything passes, even the unbearable. And yet … maybe … this is the first time that this has occurred to me … it was not love for my children that held me back, but rather my fear of dying.

Myriam came to keep me company in the kitchen and asked me if I'd like a coffee or some fruit. I chose fruit. We sat facing one another, eating. She was lost in her thoughts and I was lost in mine. Then, she stopped, looked at me tenderly, and said, "Mother, do you feel lonely?" I choked up. A tender glance alone is enough to move me, but a question like that, on top of it, caught me off guard. She continued to stare at me, while awaiting my reply. Then she asked me another poignant question,

"Are you afraid, Mother, that your children will abandon you?"

I don't like to cry in front of my children. I did it too often when they were little. Now, I'm better at controlling myself. Instead of answering the question, I found a proverb, "*When you are itchy, only your own fingernails will bring relief.*" I saw her mouthing the proverb for a few seconds as she tried to decipher it. Then she said,

"You answered my first question. And the second?" I couldn't admit that I was afraid of being abandoned by my children. She would have been disappointed that I had so little faith in life and in my children. Suddenly, an idea popped into my head, and I said,

"*Allah is on the side of the weak, to surprise the strong.*" She didn't have time to ask me what I meant. David came home from school and, a few minutes later, Véronique was also back. Saved by the bell.

Myriam wanted to drive me home. I told her that I'd rather walk, but in winter I give in more easily. It's hard to walk, especially when there is ice hidden beneath the snow. When I was young, I loved to climb over the snowbanks piled up along the sidewalks ... Myriam and the children wanted me to stay for supper and sleep over at their place. I hadn't made anything for Salim to eat and he doesn't like eating alone. I didn't tell Myriam, because she would have said that her father was a grown man and that I should start thinking about myself. Easier said than done.

I muttered something about the yogurt I was making, about having to remove the lid so that it wouldn't get too sour. Actually, the yogurt could have waited—it's even better for making *labneh* if it sits longer. But I wanted to leave. I made Véronique and David promise to come for lunch at our house the next day, just to give their mother a bit of a break. I wasn't sorry to go home, knowing that I was going to see them again the following day.

Even though I walk less and less, I still love to walk. Sometimes I think about the time when I won't be able to walk anymore. I like the neighbourhood, where I've been living since we fled Lebanon. If I'm not mistaken, I lived in Lebanon for about thirty years and have been in Canada for forty years. Now that I'm old, I have time to think—endlessly—and to count and re-count, but it never adds up to the same number. I lived in Chagour, the village where I was born, until I got married. Then I lived in Bir Barra, my husband's village, for around a dozen years. In the 1950s, we emigrated for the first time and lived in Canada for about fifteen years, after which we returned to Lebanon for ten years or so. Then the civil war broke out in Lebanon, and so we moved back to Canada.

I think I made a mistake: I spent more time there than here.

Here or there, it's all the same to me. If my children lived there, I would live there, too. Since they're here, I'm here. The only difference is the weather. You feel calmer here because of the snow, and more joyful there because of the sunshine.

For a long time, sunshine and joy were snatched from us. For a long time, people became enemies of one another, and war became the enemy of everyone.

Death and suffering ... that's what makes us all human, although sometimes I feel that many people don't deserve to be called human ... Whether they come from a rich family or a poor one, from a friendly clan or an enemy one, children are still children when they die. And the sorrow of those who are left behind—women or men, rich or poor, here or over there—is the same. I believe that death unites us and life separates us. Life highlights our differences, while death reveals what we have in common. All those who are alive can show off their power or the territory they occupy; in death, there is neither power nor territory. And having a marble gravestone won't make any difference at all. A friend's corpse will rot just as quickly as an enemy's corpse. Nothing looks more like a dead person than another dead person. Vanity is a quality of the living. Death is the same for everyone; it amounts to a breath that evaporates.

It's strange how the war around us distracts us from the war within ... When death appears on the doorstep, things fall back into perspective. Things that are unimportant fall by the wayside. We're only left with the essentials. Like not getting killed, like eating and drinking. And laughing, too.

When death is in the offing, an entire life is little more than the blink of an eye. You open your eyes, you close them, and it's all over.

I'm going to sit down and rest for a moment. My knees are struggling to prop up my body. Sometimes, I feel weak all over. When my grandchildren were little, they'd often say, "You're beautiful, *Sitto*." That would make me so happy, even though I didn't believe them. Children, like lovers, see with their hearts.

When I was young, I would wash my face over and over again. I tried to make my skin whiter by scrubbing it hard, but it just got red. If it hadn't been for how other people saw me, I might have found my face pretty. It was shiny and clear after I'd washed it so hard. In those days, men didn't have to worry about whether their skin was very dark or very pale. But women were better off if they were fair and plump. I became plump but remained dark-skinned.

For the better part of my life, I was certain that no one saw me. My mother was busy feeding us, making coffee, and serving food to the people who came to see my father. My father was busy having discussions with people, trying to restore peace in their hearts. When I was little, there were already endless casualties among the French and the Druze. My father, who was neither French nor Druze, did his best to stop the bloodshed. He believed in the power of the word and coffee helped people speak.

Much later, my husband was busy trying to earn enough money for us to survive. He was busy looking at women whom he found more beautiful than I. He was busy dealing with his frustrations, as well. He had a lot to deal with.

I opened my eyes, and soon I'll close them forever. Life has flown by too quickly. I haven't had enough time to get people to look at me, although I've tried many times.

With time, I've learned that you can't make anyone do anything. If it happens, it happens. If you love something, you look at it. That's all there is to it.

I wanted him to look at me. I wanted him to tell me, "Dounia, you're beautiful, I love you." But perhaps that wasn't done in those days, when I needed it most. Tenderness ... even today, a tender glance in my direction will flash through my body and spill out through my eyes. In that sense, age hasn't changed anything.

Like me, Salim was orphaned very young. What's more, his mother never loved him. I could never imagine a mother who didn't love her child. Maybe it was because she hardly knew him, because she hadn't raised him. Salim was still living in Lebanon when she went to live in Canada. When they met up again, he was already thirty years old, and it was a disaster. Especially because my mother-in-law was experiencing the most inhumane thing of all—her daughter falling ill and dying. Her grief left no room for anything else. Sometimes, when I think about all the pain she inflicted on us, when I'm tempted to hate her, I just remember everything she was going through. And I forgive her.

Salim and I were both orphans. He had lost his father, and I had lost my mother ... two orphans who lack tenderness and affection get married and bring children into the world, children who are orphans like them—beggars. Because an orphan can never fully grow into a father or a mother. There is no happy medium ... *scarcity is the twin of abundance ...*

Rich people used to say, "*If poor people marry one another, beggars will multiply.*" I found their disdain shocking back then, and I am still shocked. But I now know that true poverty is not what you think, and true wealth is not the kind of thing you accumulate and can count. True wealth is either there or not; it vanishes without warning and returns when it likes. You can't be proud of being rich. You carry it within yourself without recognizing its value until the day you lose it. A tiny spark, so small that it has remained nameless ...

Salim and I were not considered poor in the place where we were born. Far from it. Salim owned a lot of land, and his mother also sent him money from Canada. He lived without having to work, like a sheik. And I was the daughter of a priest … We also received money from abroad and we owned land.

I believe that Salim loved me. I think he loved me. Otherwise, why would he have come to see me so often? It took two solid hours to walk from his village to mine. He must have found me beautiful, although he never said so. Otherwise, why would he have asked for my hand in marriage? You don't marry an ugly duckling just because she's the daughter of the most respected priest in the region. He could have proposed to my sister, but no, he chose me to be his bride.

All the girls in the area would have been proud to marry him. He was handsome, his skin was fair, and he had thick, black hair. He was strong, he wasn't afraid of anything, and he had money. And he spoke well. My God, he was such a talker! He knew how to tell stories. *He could make a foreigner feel so comfortable he would forget his own country.* He charmed us with traditional stories as well as ones he made up himself. No one would ever get bored in his company. He could turn the slightest anecdote into a tale right out of the *Arabian Nights*— sometimes funny, sometimes moving, but always captivating. He made me laugh a lot. And cry, too.

Salim needed to be surrounded by people. Lots of people. It was as if he desperately wanted to be loved. It's true that he was likeable. He was totally different in a full house than he was in an empty one, with just me and the kids … When he had no one to chat with or tell stories to, he went looking for company in the village square. In Canada, there was no such thing as a village square. There were no longer people to listen to him attentively, to stare at him intently. There was no one who understood his stories. Over here, everyone goes to work and then comes home. He, too, had to work all day. Here, men go to the tavern to drink beer and watch television. Salim didn't like either beer or television. Although he managed to get by in the new languages of the country, it wasn't enough. A storyteller needs to have an excellent command of his language. Even his own children, who could have been his audience, gradually forgot their father's language as they grew older, or else lost interest in it.

His stories got stuck in his throat and choked him.

During the first years we spent here, we were both suffocating. He would look out the window, and I would stare at him. He exploded outwardly, hitting and breaking everything he touched, while I broke down inwardly, not knowing how to pour my heart out.

We could have smothered to death, but our children saved us, I think.

The first child I gave birth to on Canadian soil eventually replaced the sorrow that was choking me. She released my breath, which had become trapped in my throat. She began to take shape in my belly very soon after I arrived. She took everything. Too much for an infant. I didn't want her to live. I didn't want to let her live. May God forgive me, for I will never forgive myself.

When I think about that child in my womb, I wonder, "By what miracle did Kaokab survive, by the grace of which god has she been able to smile, talk, and laugh?"

The paths of destiny are incomprehensible at the time we are choosing which one to take, and even later on ...

Is that really a fig tree I see in the grocery store window? It wasn't there this morning ... The grocer, who is from Greece, managed to grow a fig tree in his garden, and now he has brought it into the store to keep him company ... My God, what trouble he has taken to avoid losing everything. To avoid suffering too much from everything he misses. To keep his past alive.

The grocer is smiling at me. He must have noticed how surprised I was. He points to his little fig tree, as if to say yes, it's real, alive. He is so proud ... It takes a long time before you can let go and break from the past ...

Emigrating, leaving home, leaving behind what you soon call *my* sun, *my* water, *my* fruit, *my* plants, *my* trees, *my* village. When you are in your hometown, you never say *my* sun, you say *the* sun, and you hardly talk about it since it's there, it has always been there. You don't say *my* village either, because you live there ... *Anything can become a habit, even religious devotion* ... This became clear to me when I moved from my hometown to go live in my husband's village.

The other day, I was telling Abdallah that I emigrated for the first time when I got married and went to live in Bir Barra. He really laughed. For him, emigration means changing countries, crossing oceans, and going halfway around the world. And yet, he recalled that the Prophet Muhammad is said to have emigrated from Mecca to Medina, which are two cities in the same region, where the same language is spoken. I don't know whether Muhammad felt like a migrant, but in my case I certainly did, because it was while living in my husband's village that I began to make comparisons, notice differences, experience loss and nostalgia, and long to be somewhere else without the power to go there. In short, that's where I began to feel like a foreigner.

For me, it was another country. Even though you could easily walk from one village to the other, the people were different, and, in their eyes, I was different. To them, I was an outsider, a foreigner, and also the one who had stolen Salim, who ought to have married a girl from their village. My accent wasn't the same as theirs. They didn't like what I liked, and I didn't like what they liked either. Their fruits and vegetables didn't have the same taste, the village priest was no longer my father, and I didn't recognize the landscape anymore. The village was ringed with mountains, the weather was warmer, and the air was not as fresh. The village of my childhood was perched on a mountain top, so high that

I felt I could see to the ends of the earth. Once my childhood came to an end, I never saw the horizon again. In my husband's village the mountains blocked my view. In Montreal, as in Beirut, the buildings have prevented me from seeing anything in the distance.

The only advantage was the water. The village fountain was just steps away from our house and we were allowed two jugs a day, sometimes three. When I was little, I had to walk several kilometres to fill one jug, but the water tasted so good … maybe because I was tired of walking. Here, it's even better. All you have to do is turn on the tap. Taps are amazing, and even forty years after that miraculous moment when I opened a tap for the first time, when I held my hands under clean, clear water for the first time, sometimes I still stop, look up to the heavens, and give thanks.

Since that Sunday, when I talked to my children about the nursing home, and since Myriam started asking me questions because she's worried about me, I haven't stopped thinking about my life. Usually, I think about life in general, and the life of my children and grandchildren, but rarely about my own life. Abdallah has been fine for quite a while now, Salim doesn't stay at home for very long, and that gives me time …

There are days when I'm happy. I'm in a happy place. Often, it has nothing to do with what is happening or not happening. There's no particular reason to be happy, rather than unhappy. I'm just happy, that's all.

I've learned to savour these moments the way I drink fresh water when I'm thirsty. I know that these moments will not last forever. Things can change and happiness is fleeting. *Happiness has a slippery tail* … Would this water have tasted as good if I had not been thirsty?

Whenever I think about happiness, I remember the tale of Abdo the Unhappy, a fairy tale my father used to tell some of his parishioners. If I could speak French, I'd tell the story to my grandchildren. They probably wouldn't be that interested in it at first, but they would remember the story and understand it better later on, just as I've done. I didn't hear the story all at once, because there was always an errand to run, a glass of water to fetch, or coffee to make ... I will try to piece it together to tell Abdallah when he comes around later. I will ask him to tell it to his nephews in my place.

Abdo the Unhappy was very poor. He lived in a tiny house with his wife and many children, and he found his life intolerable. He complained about his lot in life but didn't know what to do about it. One day, he had an idea. He would go see a rabbi, a priest, or an imam—I can't remember which—to ask for help. After listening to Abdo recount all his misfortunes, the man said,

"If you agree to listen to me and do everything I tell you to do, I will help you."

Abdo was willing to do anything and promised to do whatever the rabbi, the priest, or the imam told him to do.

"You have a cow," said the priest, the rabbi, or the imam.

"Yes," replied Abdo.

"Bring the cow into your house for the night," said the imam, the priest, or the rabbi.

"Into the house!" exclaimed Abdo. "That's impossible, there isn't even enough room for my family. We are all sleeping on top of each other as it is. Add a cow, too, and it will be even more unbearable."

"Do as I say and come back to see me tomorrow."

Abdo was sure that the priest, the rabbi, or the imam was out of his mind, but he did as he was told, nonetheless. The next morning, he came back even more furious than the day before.

"How many goats do you have?"

"Three."

"Tonight, you will bring all three of them inside to sleep in your house, with your cow and your family."

"That's impossible!" cried Abdo the Unhappy. "With the cow there, I didn't sleep a wink all night. With the goats, I will go crazy."

"Do as I say."

He did what he was told to do. And the story goes on to mention chickens and sheep that were brought into the house. Abdo grew more and more miserable and unhappy. Then, the rabbi, the priest, or the imam told him to take one animal out of the house each night. Abdo the Unhappy grew more joyful with each passing day, until the blessed day came when he was able to sleep with just his wife and children. That night, his house felt big, even immense, and his cares seemed very small indeed.

The unfortunate thing for Abdo the Unhappy was that he grew accustomed to his happiness too quickly ... Sometimes, when I hear someone complain—myself included—I think about that fairy tale and I take the time to savour the glass of fresh water I am drinking.

My son Abdallah came over to see us. He drops in almost every day. Of my six children and five grandchildren, he's the one who comes the most often. He lives nearby. He often invites me to his place, but I always find an excuse for not going, I don't know why. I'd rather have him come over here. He spent a long time talking to his father. When he's feeling well, he's so sweet and pleasant, so thoughtful and intelligent.

I could hear them, from a distance, talking about Quebec separating from Canada. They have held the same views for a few years: Abdallah is in favour and Salim is against. Salim says they should have proclaimed separation the night the Parti Québécois came to power in 1976, and that it's too late now. Abdallah explains to his father that Canada, unlike Lebanon, is a civilized, democratic country, where things are not done impulsively by firing a gun any old time. Instead, you have to hold a referendum. His father replied that the Québécois would never be independent, that francophones don't have the balls to do it, and that they don't have enough tough guys. Abdallah said that a country doesn't achieve independence just because it's led by a handful of tough guys, but rather because it's the will of the people.

"The people," Salim said, "the people drink their beer and watch TV! As long as people in this country can afford to buy beer, they will never change."

"This isn't like the French Revolution, when the people needed bread. Independence comes about when the people are united in a common desire to stand up and say, 'I am in my own home, I want to be able to eat whatever I want, watch TV if I want, and drink beer the way I want, without having someone come and tell me what to do.' Québécois no longer want to feel like a minority; they've been in the minority for far too long. They no longer want to rent a small room in a big house. They want to own their own home, even if it's smaller. As immigrants, we should understand what it means to not have a country of our own, to feel we are in the minority, to feel like foreigners …"

"And you think you'll feel less like a foreigner in an independent Quebec?"

"Maybe not," said Abdallah, "but I'd at least know who wanted to keep thinking of me as a foreigner. Now, I feel like a foreigner among people who feel foreign themselves, caught between two stools, neither here nor there. They're on the defensive themselves, it's harder that way."

I like to listen to them when they are not arguing. Abdallah gets a bit fired up, but he settles back down quickly. I prefer it when Salim and Abdallah talk politics rather than discussing the kind of work Abdallah might do. Salim harps on the issue all too often, though he knows full well that it only ends up upsetting everyone. Salim always seems more reasonable to me when he's discussing politics. When he delves into more personal matters, his judgment is less sound.

"When I got here," said Salim, "all the manufacturers and wholesalers I did business with spoke only English. There were no francophones running businesses, and the invoices, the names of stores, everything was in English. And yet, it was obvious to me that the people, the majority of the population, spoke French. That's why I decided to send you to French school. It was also a form of gratitude toward those back home who had welcomed our ancestors, who had taken them into their homes, or let them stay in their barns, who had saved the lives of certain people who roamed the countryside in the cold, with only a bindle slung over their shoulder and not a penny in their pockets. I wanted you to learn the language of the people first. You would learn English in the workplace in any case. The Lebanese who knew us thought I was making a bad decision, but, personally, I believed I was right. Money has never been the most important thing in my life. And besides, while they were living abroad, I had been taking part in the Lebanese independence movement. Do you remember, they all wanted you to be baptized, although you were already baptized in our faith. But for them, their religion is the only religion. If I hadn't stood my ground, you would all have gone to English schools."

"Things have changed a lot since then ..."

"As far as religion is concerned, yes, but not for the rest. They are still just as nervous, they're nothing but nervous Nellies."

"That's because they're protecting their children. What else do immigrants do? They all stick together to keep warm and cozy."

"That's normal for immigrants. They're not living on their own land."

"The Québécois aren't either. Before them, there were Indigenous Peoples, then they were conquered by the English ... and then America, surrounding them on all sides ... While we have lost our country, these people don't really have one yet ... no wonder they're cold."

"So, what are they waiting for? They should just declare their independence and be done with it!"

Salim went to his room to have a nap, and Abdallah came to keep me company in the kitchen. It was a pleasant afternoon, just the way I like it.

Abdallah told me all kinds of stories that made me laugh. He is at peace these days, thank God. If only life could always be like this … He ate a bit and helped me shell beans. And then he left. I continued to cook, alone and silent. Although there's no one left at home but Salim and me, I can't cook for just the two of us. I tell myself that given the number of children and grandchildren I have, there's a good chance that someone will drop in. If no one comes, I'll get Salim to deliver little packages of food to their place.

Just before he left, Abdallah told me that the previous night he had dreamt about our departure from the village. He'd woken up declaiming the poem he'd recited that day. He proudly remembered the little boy he'd been back then. Standing on a chair right in the middle of the village square, he'd solemnly said his goodbyes to the villagers, in his own name and on our behalf. He recalled that his teacher had helped him prepare the speech, which ended with a poem he'd written all on his own. The villagers wept. It was the first time they'd witnessed the departure of an entire family. Standing up against the kitchen door, which we'd closed so that we wouldn't wake Salim up, Abdallah recited his poem to me. For an instant, I saw him again as a twelve-year-old, small for his age, proud and standing up straight, with big, beautiful, and intelligent-looking eyes, which also revealed a deep-seated fear that has never really left him. As he spoke, his words came back to refresh my memory, brushing away the dust of time. The words were still deeply etched in my soul:

> *Oh moon, so high above, glimmering like a star*
> *The separation was to last a few days, we thought*
> *Yet, countless months and nights have now elapsed*

Abdallah was moved, as was I. His eyes were beginning to tear up, as were mine. As I watched him leave, I said to myself, "It's not a good sign when Abdallah starts remembering too much," but I quickly brushed off the thought.

Leaving for good, leaving when you know that you will never return ... what a strange feeling ... I have experienced it twice, and the third time will be the last ... I cried the first time, I cried even more the second time, and I don't yet know how many tears I'll shed for the third ...

My eyes didn't see anything anymore; my hands did only what they needed to do. There are a lot of things you have to wrap up before you leave for good. I did everything I needed to do. Children are still hungry, even on the day of departure, even if you have a fever and you feel like your heart is going to burst.

What a strange feeling. It's different from sadness, sorrow, and everyday suffering ... Losing an eye or a leg—seeing that you are in the process of losing an eye or a leg—it's not so much the wound that hurts, but rather knowing that you'll no longer have an eye or a leg, knowing that it's forever, that nothing will ever be the same as it was before ... as if you were witnessing your own death ... as if a young girl was gazing at the face she was going to have as an old woman.

Words go into hiding, like needles in a haystack.

After Abdallah recited his poem in the village square, we left. We travelled by donkey to Gharouda and then by bus to Beirut. My brother Musa—may God rest his soul—helped us out a lot by accompanying us all the way to the port of Beirut.

Abdallah and Samira led the way, followed by Samir and Farid, with Myriam and me next in line, and finally Musa, who was just behind the donkey carrying our luggage. There were five donkeys in all. I can picture it all as if it were yesterday.

Samir and Farid looked so happy, maybe because of the presents they'd received from their friends. I could hear them talking and laughing, and it comforted me. Abdallah and Samir were fighting, as usual, and Myriam was quiet, snuggled close to me.

Gharouda, the largest village in the region, was almost a city, with streets, cars, and the smell of gasoline. About a dozen years earlier, I'd gone there with my brother and sister to have my wedding dress made. But it was the first time I'd set foot in Beirut. When I saw the narrow streets overflowing with people, without a single deserted spot, without greenery, with its oppressive heat, humidity, and unbearable stench, I thought that if I'd had to live in the city, I would never have had children. Cities aren't made for children—and I still believe that today.

Since the ship wasn't sailing until the next morning, we had to spend the night in a hotel. What a hotel it was! I was really happy that my brother had come with us. Located right in the centre of town, the hotel and the streets around it were populated with low-priced prostitutes, as I found out afterward, when I went back to live in Lebanon.

Today, after fifteen years of war, there is nothing left of that hotel, or the street it was on, or even the city centre ...

The crossing took twenty days. Twenty days on board with five children aged four to twelve, without knowing one word of any of the languages people spoke, with a two-day stopover and change of ship, and just a few coins in our pockets. I don't know how I did it ... The children played and got dirty, even on a large, clean ship. Everything was smooth and white onboard, except the long corridor in the hold leading to our cabin. That's where the children would play. The floor, all the way up to the inside of our cabin, was covered with a red substance that stuck to their clothes. It's easy to do laundry with your own two hands, but if you can't speak the language, don't know how to find the soap, or where to wash the clothes, or hang them out to dry ... not to mention being seasick ... Oh, I don't know how I did it ... *God is on the side of the weak, to surprise the strong* ... I had to do it, so I did it. I waved my hands around, I made faces, and I made people laugh, which is better than making them cry. Food was not a problem—everything was taken care of. We ate new and different foods every day, in a beautiful white dining room. It was all aglow with electric lights that glittered as if they were throwing a party three times a day. A tall, blond young man came to sit with us almost all the time. He was friendly and cheerful, and helped the little ones to eat with cutlery, which was new to them. I never learned the name of the young man because I didn't speak to him, but in my heart, I thank him each time his image flashes through my head.

Abdallah helped me a lot. He knew how to read and write, he was smart, and he gave me good advice. We needed one another. Together, we were less afraid. Without him, I would never have left home.

I would rather have stayed in the village with my children and continued to receive the money that their father sent from overseas. But Salim persisted and sent letter after letter. Abdallah would read them to me twice—rather than just once—to make sure that I understood. Salim said that he was lonely, that he didn't have enough money to come back home, and that he couldn't go on living without us. I didn't feel the same. I've never felt better than during the two years I spent alone with the kids.

They were peaceful years, a time we enjoyed together. I knew full well what awaited me over there. I'd heard all about it. Before he became a priest my father had gone there twice, my father-in-law had made three trips over, and other men had done the same. Women, too, but I hadn't met any who'd come back.

In those days, I could read between the lines, so to speak. Of course, they had money when they came back, but money isn't everything. Not having a place to sleep, night after night, sleeping in barns just to avoid being out in the cold, wandering from house to house, in summer and winter, with just a bindle tied to a stick carried over their shoulder, speaking their own language only when they came to the city for supplies. And the cold, the silence, the longing for their family, friends, and everything they had once known.

Besides, those men didn't have children. I had five. It's even more difficult with children. Of course, it's also easier, in other ways.

I knew what awaited me ... *even if you can't see it with your own eyes, you can imagine it ...*

I went anyway. I relented. I learned to give in. One day, my daughter—I think it was Kaokab—said, "Mother, you often give in, but you don't break." That surprised me. Personally, I feel that I've been broken many times. Into a thousand pieces. Sometimes, I wonder how I can still smile and laugh out loud.

Life is so short. Up to the age of thirty, I believed the world ended at Gharouda, which was three villages over from ours. When I arrived in Beirut to board the ship, I realized that there was more to the world. We crossed the sea. I learned later that the body of water we sailed across was called the Mediterranean. I'd often heard the name in stories. In Italy, we changed ships. The world kept getting bigger and bigger, while I seemed to grow smaller and smaller. And then, there was nothing else to look at but water and sky. It was the Atlantic Ocean. One single name for all of that! I have one name, and the ocean also has just one.

After twenty days at sea, we landed in Halifax. Salim had come to pick us up. It had been almost two years since we'd seen him. He was so happy. Five children to kiss at the same time. He really loves his children. I don't know how he could have lived without them for two years.

We took the train. It was the first time I'd travelled by train. I was doing and seeing everything for the first time. A woman who believes that the entire world ends three villages away from her own has many things to learn, to see, and to understand.

As the train rolled into Montreal, the world kept stretching out farther and farther. Does the world end somewhere? There are so many things I don't know ... Life, the one allotted to each of us, is so short ... and the world is so vast ...

Salim became obsessed with finding work for Abdallah. Together, they went to see Salim's cousin, who supposedly had a job for him. I told Salim that it was pointless, since Abdallah wasn't able to hold down a job for more than a week or two. I urged him to accept his son the way he was, once and for all. I think that Salim can't distinguish between his wishes and reality. He's incapable of putting himself in someone else's shoes. For him, Abdallah is just lazy and spineless, which is easier to deal with than illness … *A person who is not affected by words, will not even be affected by the sword* … In fifty years of marriage, I've never managed to make him change his mind about anything. I often wonder what purpose I serve. Any discussion soon turns into an argument. Salim and I sometimes chat over coffee, but we rarely have a meaningful conversation. As soon as he sees that my opinions are different from his, he gets angry and raises his voice, while I keep quiet. He loves to get into discussions with strangers, so why doesn't he ever discuss things with me? When he's with other people, he listens and shares his thoughts, but with me, he doesn't hear what I tell him and, in any case, he always thinks he's right. You might as well be talking to a wall.

Often, when he's with others, I hear him singing the praises of motherhood with clichés such as "mother of the universe," "centre of the world," "mother of giving and forgiving," and other nonsense like that. It makes me laugh. If I understand him correctly, the centre of the universe should be immobile and silent while those who revolve around it can talk, move about, and do as they please.

Anyway ...

I think that Salim is jealous of the attention I lavish on my children. I've never complained about it, because I'm sure he can't help it. He's just jealous, even though he loves his children as much as I do.

Jealousy! God, how I suffered from it when I was young. Just the thought that Salim might have spoken to another woman, touched her, laughed with her—all of that was pure torture. I tried to talk myself out of it, but it was beyond my control. It took years for me to get over those feelings, and then they just faded away. Today, I could never be jealous in that way; it causes a lot of pain for nothing. Old age—no matter what I think about it sometimes—has advantages after all.

Salim's jealousy is less intense than mine was. You couldn't even call it jealousy. It's attention that he needs but is not getting. It's true that I am more concerned about the children's well-being than I am about his. I admit it. But I can't help it.

At times, I feel as if I hate Salim as much as I once loved him. Deep-seated bitterness—I don't even know where it comes from—casts a shadow over my feelings. I try to control it as best I can, but it still comes through and tarnishes my actions. At other times, I do everything I can to make him happy. My efforts sink into the void like dead birds. Then I stop trying for a long while. Does he ever do anything for me?

Never the slightest gesture, no signs of affection—he's even jealous of the affection my children and grandchildren have for me. The kids often forget his birthday, but they always remember mine. He says that it doesn't bother him, but that's impossible, it couldn't be true. When you are two steps away from the grave, the smallest sign of affection is like a spray of fragrant flowers.

Anyway …

Life is too short to spend your time arguing. People in Salim's village, and later my mother-in-law, enjoyed arguing. And it's still Salim's favourite pastime. I've been really unlucky. Even after fifty years of marriage, I'm still not used to it. I would tell myself, "Don't listen, let them argue, and even if it's directed at you, let it go … *If you make things difficult, they will be difficult; if you make them easy, they will become easy …*" I would repeat those words, and then calm down a little, but to make everything easy and normal, I'd have to crawl back into my mother's womb and be born again.

You can't turn back the clock, I know, but the best meal in the world, even a feast, tastes sour if the people around the table are argumentative or in a bad mood while you're eating. I'd just as soon dine on bread and olives, as long as I could do so in peace.

Since we've grown old, Salim has been trying to convince me that quarrelling is better than being bored, that it's better to spill your guts right away, and that a bit of fighting is just like a game. No matter how hard I try, I'm not able to do it. I feel like one of those bad actors you see on television. Salim, on the other hand, is like a good actor—he can make me forget that he's just acting.

Serenity and peace of mind. That's what I wish people when I greet them, and it's what I'd like them to wish for me.

Salim gets up early. He's always gotten up before me. That hasn't changed since we were first married. As soon as he opens his eyes, he gets out of bed and makes himself a coffee. He has never criticized me for getting up later, nor have I reproached him for getting up earlier. I can say that it's the only thing in our life that's gone well, in an orderly fashion, with respect for the other person.

It's the time of day I love the most. Lying in my bed alone, warm and cozy, half awake, half asleep, I smell the aroma of coffee, which is faint at first, then stronger. My eyes open fully, and I gaze at the tree outside my window.

When the children were little, I didn't remain in that state for very long, but since getting old—except for the times when Abdallah isn't well—I can savour these moments as much as I like. Sometimes I doze off as the aroma of coffee drifts up into my nostrils. When I wake up again, the scent of coffee has faded away, there is no more noise, no sense of time passing. I lie there, motionless, with my eyes closed, barely breathing.

Before, I didn't really have the time to experience moments like these. With six children, a mother has no time for herself. She experiences pleasure when everyone else is happy. Seven other people come before her, not counting the grandmother or cousins who come for a few days and end up staying for months.

Now, I can take my time. I am confronting death. I take all the time I need to try to feel what it will be like to no longer feel anything …

Just as a child must learn to walk, an old person must learn to die. I should still have a few years left, and if God extends my life a little, I will eventually learn. I already know that I will miss the aroma of coffee. I will miss this tree, too, the one I see when I first open my eyes … and the sound of my grandchildren laughing.

We'd been living in Sainte-Thérèse for about a year. We were staying with my mother-in-law, in the suite above her store. There wasn't a single day of joy or even serenity. Not one day went by without a fight: my mother-in-law fought with Salim, Salim fought with me and the children, the children fought with each other. I silently tormented myself, feeling sorry that I hadn't stayed back in the village with my children. And now we were leaving again. Even if all the devils in hell had conspired to make our lives unlivable, I should never have agreed to leave my mother-in-law's home under those circumstances. When I think back on it now, I realize that my mother-in-law must not have been in her right mind to do such a thing—throwing an entire family out on the street! When someone's heart has begun to harden, there's no telling how far they'll go.

I packed the large trunk and rolled up the carpet my family had given me when I got married, which was my sole possession. Salim went out to find a taxi and we all piled in.

We had to find a place before nightfall. We had to rent a house …

Allah never closes all doors at once … But blinded by pain and despair, you don't even see the tiniest door. It was summertime, thank God, it was summer …

The children had just completed their first year of school. It was around seven o'clock in the evening and we'd almost finished eating supper. I've never understood why some people choose the dinner hour to argue with each other. It's as if they had no respect for the food they were served. It was like that in my husband's family, whereas in my family people laughed and were in good spirits. It's perhaps the laughter I stored away during my childhood that helped me endure the tears that flowed later. My father had a jolly temperament, he loved to laugh and make jokes. He was not at all stern like other priests. One day during Lent, he saw me getting dressed to go to Mass with him. I had just woken up and was still rubbing my eyes. He said to me, "Go back to bed, little one, God doesn't need your prayers, he has his angels and saints. Sleep a little longer, you have a lot of things to do today, and your sister-in-law needs your help."

Ever since I was little, there's always been someone who has needed my help. And yet, how many times in my life have I tried to cry out for help only to have no one come to the rescue? I've always had to figure things out for myself, gradually learning how to untangle the knots in my throat. For a long time, I resented the entire world and was particularly annoyed with those who could have helped but didn't. But today, I'm at an age when it's easier to forgive, although I would like to reach the point where I could also understand.

If I've been able to forgive even before understanding, it's because I know that hate, resentment, bitterness, and rancour are not good for the body or soul …

As we drove past the church in Sainte-Thérèse, I thought of my mother and made the sign of the cross. The children were all quiet, miraculously. Salim was breathing heavily and with some difficulty. His eyebrows were knitted together, his forehead was furrowed, and his Adam's apple was bobbing up and down. I couldn't see the inside of his throat, but I'm sure he had knots in it. I think that I did too, but I don't remember. I just remember that I was going to wake up …

Twenty or thirty years ago, I thought that my mother-in-law was a nasty, heartless woman. That may well be true, but now I think that Salim and I were just fools … *Everyone relies on their own intelligence to plant their orchard* … We should have stayed at my mother-in-law's until the next morning, at least. One more fight wouldn't have changed our life in any way. Salim could have gone to look for a house alone, and then we could have moved after that, in peace.

Salim has never taken the time to stop, have a look, think, consider things calmly, and then make a decision. He gets carried away, as if rearing onto his hind legs like the horses you see in cowboy movies. Salim is a cowboy, while I'm the woman in the saloon who washes the dishes and glasses behind the bar. I've lost everything over the years—even my will power.

Today, with both feet planted firmly on the ground, I would say no. It's so easy to say so after the fact, but to do it at the very moment the movie of your life is playing, when you are in the thick of the action …

We drove through small towns and villages. We passed houses that were all spread out, far from each other. I can still hear the silence. There was no one outside and no houses for rent. A nightmare in slow motion, without a word, without a sound. The baby was asleep in my arms, and the children were leaning up against me in the back seat of the car. Abdallah was seated up front, between his father and the taxi driver.

It wasn't sleeping outdoors that worried me the most. It was Abdallah. Salim and I were old enough to withstand such a situation, and the little ones were too young to notice, but Abdallah was neither old nor young. He understood too much and not enough. I was afraid of the harm this would do to him. I can still picture his little head held high and his slim neck. He never leaned against his father's shoulder, and he didn't rest his head on the car seat. He did nothing to wipe away his tears. Maybe he wasn't crying. He remained alert, reading everything he saw in writing.

There was nothing to rent.

When we reached Terrebonne, all the children were asleep, except Abdallah who was holding his head up even straighter, with his neck stretched out even farther. We'd cruised up and down the streets, one after the other. This was the town in which Salim had rented a store two days earlier. I don't know where he'd found the money. It didn't come from his mother—that was what most of their arguments were about. Perhaps he'd convinced the wholesalers to give him credit. Salim has some admirable qualities—he is honest and inspires trust. Besides, I believe there's a guardian angel to watch over large families such as ours …

It was dark out. Abdallah spotted a sign that read: HOUSE FOR RENT. Salim jumped out of the car and went to knock on the door. Salim knocked louder and louder, so loud that he woke up the neighbours. The owner lived three houses down. When he saw a whole family jammed into a taxi, wanting to rent his summer home, at midnight, he thought he must be dreaming. He went to get his keys, and then he even lowered the rent.

The house was large, damp, and almost empty. There was only one lightbulb still hanging from the kitchen ceiling. We unrolled the carpet. I lined the children up on the rug. Then, I lay down at one end, with their father at the other end. I had rolled up some clothes to make pillows.

In the dark, I heard Abdallah say to his father, "Thank God, we have a roof over our heads." Usually, it's the parents who thank God, not the children.

My son was right, we could have been sleeping out on the sidewalk. The cab driver wouldn't have let us spend the whole night in his car. I wonder what we would have done if Salim hadn't had a bit of money, or if it had been winter instead of summer.

I didn't mind sleeping on the floor as it wasn't cold. The first time I ever slept in a bed, I was afraid of falling out. It was in Gharouda, the time I went to have my wedding dress made. My brother, my sister, and I stayed with friends of my father. They had a beautiful house on a hilltop, with beds, indoor toilets, and a very white sink. I liked the sink and the toilet, but not the bed.

Dogs bark whereas humans adapt ... When we stayed with my mother-in-law, it took me a year to get used to sleeping in a bed, and then I began to find the floor hard. That wasn't the hardest part, though. I didn't want the sun to rise. I wanted to sleep forever and never wake up again. Sometimes your eyes don't fill with tears right away. You have to wait a while, and rest. Even tears need time to rest.

That night, I had one of those dreams that come back often. It's always the same dream, but the place changes. I'm walking around with a baby in my arms and then I'm crying while looking for my baby, whom I can't find ... I wake up crying, sometimes sitting up in bed, sometimes wandering around the house.

I remember my dream, but not what we had to eat the next day. Did Salim go out to buy bread? Did I have enough milk for my baby? Was she crying? That morning, I know, I was sorry that I wasn't breastfeeding this time. The doctor had told me not to nurse her. I followed his advice because I thought everything was different over here. What was good enough for my five children over there, I thought, wouldn't be good for my youngest child, because she was born here. I felt like I couldn't tell right from wrong anymore, I couldn't think or make decisions anymore, and I didn't know anything at all anymore. I'd almost forgotten my own name ...

We must have eaten that day and for days afterward, because we didn't starve to death. I remember that Salim went to work in the store. He took Abdallah and Samira with him to help out.

They say that a tiny trickle of spring water is better than a lake that's running dry. The four hundred dollars that Salim's cousin had lent him weren't going to last forever. The rent was paid up until September and a lot of money had been spent on the taxi, so the store had to be up and running as quickly as possible. I don't know how Salim managed to rent the store. All I know is that we had a store on Main Street and a roof over our heads on Wellington, with one light bulb, a large wood stove without wood, an icebox without ice, an old pot, one table, two chairs, but no glasses and no plates. Water flowed from the tap, which made it easier to get than going to collect it at a fountain.

The children would play on the porch, which was wrapped almost all the way around the house. I've always found porches beautiful. You can be both indoors and outdoors at the same time. It's a good thing that there are so many of them in this country. Otherwise, people wouldn't see one another very much.

As I watched the children play, I wondered: How do they do it? I'm amazed that nothing stops children from playing.

It was a summer house. I didn't yet know what that meant, and I was afraid of winter. For me, a house was a house. You live there your whole life. First, your parents' house, then your husband's house, which becomes your house if everything goes well with the husband. When you change countries, you also have to change everything you know about life. You have to learn quickly. That has never bothered me. Actually, I like to learn new things.

"When you live in Canada, you have to keep both your bathing suit and your fur coat close at hand, always ready and not too far from each other," said those who came back to the village. We used to laugh because we didn't wear either bathing suits or fur coats in the village. We didn't understand. Once I lived in this summer home, I understood. That year, the weather changed drastically. The swings in temperature were so sudden and so unexpected that you didn't need a fur coat, perhaps, but warm clothes were a must in any case. Only to take them off several hours later ... I didn't yet wear a bathing suit ... *After forty days, you either behave as they do or you leave* ... that's what they say, but it took me a little longer to put on a bathing suit.

We were camping, a bit like the Bedouins who travelled through our villages for a few days each year. Unlike the

Bedouins, who had to pitch their tents and take them down again, we had our big summer house, which provided shelter from the rain, but not always the cold and damp weather.

It was nearly September. We could feel that a harsh winter was coming. Salim spoke to the owners of the store, and they took us in. They lived behind Salim's store and worked in their movie theatre right next door. Their living quarters were on three floors, comprising a finished basement that was part of the movie theatre, a kitchen and living room at street level, and three large bedrooms on the second floor. They let us have the kitchen and living room, which overlooked the store, and one of the upstairs bedrooms. They kept two bedrooms and the basement for themselves. They had to walk through our kitchen to reach their bedrooms.

Even relatives wouldn't have done more for us. Monsieur and Madame Archambault, and Madame Morin, Madame Archambault's sister, were like angels to us. They welcomed us into their home, and it cost less to rent than the big, cold house. It was also more convenient, since Salim was able to eat his meals without leaving the store.

When I think about Monsieur and Madame Archambault and Madame Morin, I am convinced that they're the best people I've ever met. They were so kind, and they weren't even Lebanese. When they compare themselves to people here, the Lebanese like to brag about their generosity, a trait that is part of our tradition, it's true. What they fail to see is that the generosity of people here is more discreet, stemming from a genuine desire to do good rather than from a need to look good. For me, kindness is worth more than generosity because it has nothing to do with social conventions. The actions of Monsieur and Madame Archambault and Madame Morin were not driven by a wish to be well regarded by their friends, but rather by the goodness of their hearts.

Monsieur and Madame Archambault and Madame Morin must be dead by now, as they were already elderly back then. May they rest in peace. I am eternally grateful to them. Sometimes, I mention their names to my children, just to keep their memory alive.

Six children and two adults living in one bedroom, a small living room, and a tiny kitchen. I thanked my lucky stars for schooldays when there were just two of them left at home. But rainy Saturdays and Sundays—I'd just as soon forget about them!

I did my best not to disturb our three guardian angels, to let them live their lives in peace. *If your good friends were made of honey, you wouldn't devour them all at once ...* It even makes sense for angels.

The lack of space was easier to take than the noise. When Salim scolded the children, he would make noise. If the punishment didn't quite alleviate his frustrations or quiet the boys down, there was even more noise! A glance, a hint of displeasure from our hosts, and my stomach would be tied in knots.

In those days, I realized that it was better to live in your own garret than in someone else's castle. It wasn't that Monsieur and Madame Archambault were nosy—they were so discreet going up and down the stairs—but we were living with them, in their home, and that was something we couldn't ignore. It was also hard to keep the kids from running around as much as they would have liked.

The landlords never complained. I was the one who couldn't take it any longer. The situation didn't seem to get on Salim's nerves or bother the children either. That's normal at their age. I was the only one who thought about the well-being of our hosts.

If only I could have spoken to them ... I could say hello, I knew that word at least. I managed to smile at them, and a smile is a smile in any language. They could tell that I wasn't mute, but I would have liked to be deaf, mute, and blind. That would have been easier, because I had to behave as if I actually were.

Eventually, our three guardian angels realized that living with six young children, a father who often burst into fits of anger, and a mother who worked from morning to night, barely touching the walls as she tiptoed about—all that was beyond what their strength and kindness could bear. Not to mention Salim's friends who would come to visit us and sometimes stay for weeks or even months, since he did everything in his power to keep them there. Poor Salim! He had such a need to talk and have a good time that he practically begged them to stay on.

When I look back on all that, I wonder how we managed to live cheek by jowl like that. How did I get enough air to breathe? Suddenly the answer occurs to me, and I picture an unusually lively and tiny lady with grey hair—Madame Chevrette. If Monsieur and Madame Archambault were our guardian angels at the time, Madame Chevrette was our sunshine. Mine, in particular.

Madame Chevrette was the first saleslady to work in Salim's store. Later, there were other ones, but Madame Chevrette was the funniest, the toughest, the most honest, and the most loyal. It was thanks to her that we were able to build up a clientèle. The neighbourhood women would come in to say hello when they were passing by and didn't leave the store without buying all kinds of things. She was a very good salesperson, and she loved us so much. We all loved her very much, too. After school, my children would drop in to see Madame Chevrette first. Sometimes, she would help them with their assignments and homework. She took on what we were incapable of doing, given our ignorance. Abdallah and Samira sometimes filled in for her on Saturdays.

The other day, Abdallah told me that "chevrette" means "a little goat." I was pleased to learn that, as goats are my favourite animal. If it had been up to me to give her a name, I couldn't have found a more suitable one.

Salim trusted her utterly. He would go to Montreal for days to buy supplies and would leave the store in her hands. Madame Chevrette was fifty-nine years old, the combined age of Salim and me. She was a mother to us all. She wanted the best for us, just like parents who want only the best for their own children.

She was the one who taught me the few words of French I know, which I will never forget because she taught me so well. She made a lot of faces and used grimaces, gestures, and even games so that I would understand. She put her heart and soul into it, so much so that I eventually understood something. I learned the French words for banana, sandwich, butter, bread, tomato, and eat, along with basic expressions like "I'm not hungry today," "the baby is crying," "the children," "good," and "not good." She even taught me how to count in French. She often said, "*C'est donc de valeur, c'est bien de valeur,*" with a different expression on her face each time. I never did get what she meant, and neither did Abdallah, who knows both Arabic and French very well.

I have never seen anyone so even-tempered. I'd forgotten that it was possible to be happy to be alive. Quite innocently. On the days when Salim went to Montreal to do his shopping, everything felt calm and peaceful. We would talk, often by using hand gestures, and we understood each other. I would sit between the kitchen door and the first counter, with my baby in my arms, watching customers come into the store. They would speak to Madame Chevrette and finally leave after buying a few odd things, the purpose of which was unclear to me. But we were making money ... Every day, Madame Chevrette ate the same thing for lunch, for months and months on end, and it didn't seem to bother her. She would have two slices of buttered white bread with a banana and a 7 Up, which she carried in the same brown paper bag that she folded back up after lunch and brought home with her to use again the next day. Every once in a while, she would eat a tomato instead of the banana and a small can of sardines, which looked like a feast judging from the way she opened her bag and said to me, "Do you want to taste some sardines, Madame Dounia?" No one had ever attached the word "madame" to my given name. Customarily, the family name of the husband takes precedence, and in Lebanon I was also called *Uum Abdallah*, Abdallah's mother. Madame Chevrette pronounced my name so lovingly and respectfully that I felt like an extraordinary woman, for one day a week at least.

Sometimes, when I had leftovers from something delicious I'd made the previous night, I would offer her some. She would put her sandwich aside and taste the food, exclaiming enthusiastically but eating very little. She thanked me so profusely that I was embarrassed. That's what I find remarkable in the people here: they are grateful for the slightest favour.

Kaokab, my youngest, came to pick me up and drive me to her house. She wanted me to teach her how to cook zucchini with yogurt, which she loves. I would have preferred that she come to my house, but she insisted that I go there, so I gave in. Just as we were arriving at her place, the telephone rang once, then a second time, and then a third. As a result, I was just sitting there waiting.

When I go to my children's homes, especially the ones I visit often, I feel at home. Now that I'm old, I'm comfortable most anywhere. When I go to the home of strangers, which is rare, I'm just visiting and it's not the same. I stay in the living room, I listen to people talk, and I sometimes utter a few words. With my children, I can spend an hour or an entire day, or even stay for ten days. I make myself at home as soon as I get there. I don't stay in the living room. I cook, especially dishes they don't know how to make themselves, and I wash the dishes, even if they tell me to rest. Sometimes, I do nothing. I look out the window, I watch them live their lives, and I laugh with my grandchildren. They teach me new words, and I go out of my way to pronounce them badly just so I can hear them laughing.

I don't feel like a stranger; I feel like I belong in their household. Salim is just the opposite. Fifteen minutes after getting there, he already wants to leave. He can never just sit and do nothing. He's never relaxed anywhere and even the children sense it. I would really like Salim to be happy ...

As I grow older, I don't need much anymore. Looking out the window, thinking, breathing. That's enough and I'm never bored. Or almost never. I don't why I felt so emotional when Myriam asked me if I was lonely.

On occasion, I meet their friends. My children introduce me and say proudly, "This is my mother." Their friends speak to me a bit, but as I can't really reply, my children come to my rescue and change the subject, after which I feel liberated.

But I still sit close by and watch them. I really like to meet the friends of my children, but what I enjoy even more, is seeing my children interacting with their friends. When they were young, they never invited anyone over to the house. Perhaps they were ashamed of us. I never saw them talking or playing with anyone who wasn't a member of the family. Even though they spoke a language different from my own when they talked with each other, I didn't yet notice the distance between us.

At the time, I didn't have the luxury to think about all these things. I had too much work to do. Maybe I was just too consumed with an insidious ailment that affected my head and heart. It ate away at me, even on good days when everything seemed fine. I missed the sunshine, I think. Back in Lebanon, we did everything outdoors rather than staying cooped up within four walls. Sure, we stayed in the house in winter, but it was so short. I don't know how that dark mood dissipated, nor at what moment I started noticing that there was a sky here, too, and that it was sometimes quite blue and very beautiful. It took me around ten years, I think. Ten years without a sky—that's a long time.

For a few years now, I've had the time to "philosophize," as Salim says when he wants to tease me. And why wouldn't

I have the right to philosophize given that I have lived for three-quarters of a century?

It's mostly when my children are with their friends that I notice the gap that has developed between them and me. Every time—and it happens when I least expect it—I ask myself the same question when someone is laughing or speaking in a language that I don't understand. Is that really my son or daughter? Can I really be their mother?

It's true that my children came out of my womb and that I nourished them with milk from my breasts. But apart from the obvious, in what way am I their mother? Am I their mother because I love them, and they love me? I love the tree growing slowly outside my window. I love the birds and watch them every day from my bedroom window. They are beautiful and I love them … But loving is not enough. There is surely something else, but I can't figure out what it could be. If I had adopted the children instead of giving birth to them, would I still be their mother? In case of extreme danger, a matter of life or death, would I give my life for one of my children? I think so, but as I've never had to do it, I don't know how I'd act in those circumstances. Every time such thoughts cross my mind, I think about the cat that was locked in an oven with her kitten. The heat rose gradually from the bottom element. At first, the cat protected her kitten. She took it between her teeth and put it on her back. When the heat became unbearable, the mother cat climbed onto her kitten's back, putting it under her paws so that she wouldn't get burned herself …

Would I give my life for one of my children?

If Kaokab keeps talking on the phone, you can kiss the zucchini goodbye! I don't know how she manages to talk so much. She must be exhausted!

In the villages, people would drop in at your house at any time. Here, people telephone at any time of the day or night, for no particular reason …

I could have started by myself, but she told me not to. She wants to see everything, my every move. It's not rocket science, after all—it's just zucchini with yogurt.

Anyway …

I don't often go to Kaokab's place. She used to live with girlfriends, and then with men. I've always made a point of turning down her invitations without letting on that I felt uncomfortable. I'm too shy to go to the homes of people I don't know. Now that she's a teacher, she has a nice apartment all to herself. Her current boyfriend must be living with her … I'll get used to the idea eventually … Before inviting me, she makes sure to say, "I'm going to be alone today." She understands that I'm not comfortable with her living arrangements, but I never have to say anything. It would be a lot easier if she got married …

Anyway …

It's the same with Farid. I never know who's going to walk out of his bedroom. In any case, Farid never invites me to his place, and it's better that way, because I get a bit bored in his company. He doesn't talk, and his silence and reserve throw me back into a state that I have experienced before—it's like a desert that is neither hot nor cold, where I no longer know who I am, where I will die, and no one will come to bury me … where even death doesn't matter to me …

Anyway …

With Kaokab, it's exactly the opposite. Just hearing her laugh cheers me up, even though I might have been better off staying home today. If we'd been at my house, the zucchini would have been half cooked by now …

Perhaps I could begin to count her books … It would take me a whole day to count them, and at least ten lifetimes to read them … Entire walls full of books, just like at Myriam's. Where has she found the time to read all that stuff, when she's always on the run?

With all these books, all these words, all these thoughts, and all these stories, how come the world is not in better shape? That's what I wonder every time I see so many books all at once. Maybe those who are causing the problems don't read, because they're so busy doing harm … But then, what are all those books for?

One day, for a reason that escapes me now, my father asked me,

"Do you know how to read, Dounia?"

"No, Father," I replied.

"What? You don't know the letters of the alphabet?"

I said, "Yes, I know the alphabet."

"Well, then," he said, "you know how to read. Words are composed of letters placed one after the other, and sentences are made up of a series of words. Pick up a newspaper and read."

A parishioner came in, and that put an end to the reading lesson. My father didn't even realize that I wasn't going to school anymore and he didn't encourage me to do so. It's easy to say, "Pick up the paper and read." It takes me an hour to decipher a single line, and by the time I get to the third word, I've already forgotten the first one … One day, I ran away from school to avoid a beating. I was so afraid of the teacher, a man who whipped us furiously with a completely clear conscience … and that was to make us learn more! And I wasn't very gifted. Basically, it suited everyone, including me, to stop going. I preferred to look after Musa's children because my sister-in-law had too much to do … and go to work in the fields at harvest time.

I would never even have noticed that I was ignorant if we hadn't emigrated. Back home, books didn't line the walls the way they do in the homes of my girls. My father had a few of them tucked away in a cabinet in his bedroom, along with some religious objects—that's all.

My father often spoke to us about Ibn Arabi, Omar ibn al-Khattab, Sultan Rashid, the Prophet Muhammad, Jesus and his mother, Mary Magdalene, and many others. It was marvellous because even though all those people have been dead for a long time, what they said or did has been passed down through the ages …

I don't remember all the stories in detail, but I have retained fragments of them without having made any particular effort or having had a teacher to hit me. There was one about the meaning of justice, which impressed me when I was little and continues to impress me. Why do I remember that story and not others? If life is a mystery to me, memory is the mystery of all mysteries.

Omar ibn al-Khattab—I believe he's the one. My father liked him a lot because he remained humble and close to the people even though he was powerful. In fact, it's not important to know who it was, whether it was Omar, or Jesus, or someone whose name has been forgotten. What matters is that their actions and words still warm our hearts and enlighten our minds.

A mosque in Syria or Iraq—I no longer know exactly where it was—needed to be expanded. To do this, they had to demolish the house of an old man, who was of the Jewish faith, I believe. But the man loved his house and neighbourhood and didn't want to leave, even if he were compensated generously. So, the man went to see Omar, the Emir of the Faithful, and told him everything. It was clear to Omar that the old man was in the right. He ordered that everything be stopped, and said these words, which my father would often repeat, "Let the mosque fall to pieces, but never let justice die." A man as wise as Omar would not agree to a place of worship being built on a site of injustice perpetrated against one man. He probably thought it was just as easy to build the mosque elsewhere.

If the Jews who came to take away the homes of Palestinians when I was young, and even after I grew up, had heard this story, perhaps they wouldn't have done what they did. I say what the Jews did to the Palestinians, but I could also have said the Turks to the Armenians, the Germans to the Jews, the Iraqis to the Kurds, the Americans to the Iraqis or the Vietnamese before that, the English and the French to the Indigenous Peoples of North America, or the Whites to the Blacks. There are many other examples.

All I know about the history of human beings, I heard from my father, from Salim, from Abdallah, and sometimes from the radio or television. People don't change much, but they do somewhat. There are no longer any slaves—you can't buy a person the way you would buy a sack of potatoes. But there are many people who are so hungry that they would sell themselves. Women and children have more rights than they once did, to some extent. Nowadays, you could say that a woman is equal to a man, and that a child is a person ...

What I like about Salim is that he reads a lot and tells me what's going on in the world. Abdallah, too, talks to me a lot, in his calmer moments. He brings me up to date and teaches me. All my children and grandchildren teach me things, each one in their own way. I also have television, which allows me to see countries that I would never be able to visit, along with animals, fish, birds, the bottom of the ocean, and other planets ...

Kaokab apologized twenty times, she kissed me thirty times, and she made me laugh. I've already forgiven her. If she hadn't been my daughter, I would have gotten up and left long since ... I just told her that answering machines were sometimes quite useful, and that Myriam was very pleased with hers.

"I do want one, I just haven't gotten around to it yet," she replied.

My daughter Kaokab is a modern young woman, as they say. She is always running from one place to the next, and never has time. My children are all modern, each one in a particular way. They all seem to be chasing something that moves faster than they do when they are moving fast, that slows down when they slow down, something elusive and fleeting, with a tail more slippery than the tail of happiness.

Kaokab poured me a small glass of sweet wine—she calls it an *apéritif*—but I have a feeling that there will be no follow-up to the apéritif, because the zucchini is a long way from the stove. It still needs to be blanched, hollowed out, and rubbed with garlic on the inside. Then, you make the stuffing with meat that has been finely minced by hand instead of in a meat grinder. You stuff the zucchini and then prepare the yogurt, cooking it while stirring constantly so that there are no lumps. And the yogurt is not even made—it takes three or four hours to ferment.

Kaokab had a mischievous look on her face as she came back from the kitchen carrying a container of commercial yogurt in each hand. Modern life certainly has its advantages. I've never cooked with store-bought yogurt before. With Kaokab, anything can happen!

The store was doing well, thank God. Salim was working very hard, and Madame Chevrette was a big help. We were able to rent a house with three small bedrooms, a living room, a kitchen, and a basement with a concrete floor where the children could play. It wasn't a palace, but the children were able to run around without disturbing anyone. The weather was beautiful that summer. I planted vegetables in the backyard and watered my tomatoes and parsley with a rubber hose. I could turn on the tap, pull the hose over gently, and get all the water I needed. What a dream come true for a former mountain girl, and still a mountain girl at heart.

Each time we moved, things improved. We lived in seven different houses in fifteen years. I never hung curtains in the windows of any of the houses. It was a dream, though, a small, simple dream. It's not that I love curtains. They gather dust, and dust isn't good for your health. But for me, in those days, having curtains on your windows meant that you were settling in for good. Like everyone else, you belonged to the country and were beginning to feel at home. It seemed to me that if we could finally hang curtains, we would be happy.

In my mind, curtains were different from everything I had experienced until then—the most different. I saw them everywhere, even on television shows like *Father Knows Best* and *La famille Plouffe*. Even Jackie Gleason had them. But we never did. The time to buy them never came. We always moved before that, and Salim would say that it was a waste of money since we were soon going back to live in Lebanon ... To console myself, I would think, "All the other houses have curtains, which they close in the evening, so nobody can see us."

I admired French Canadians, or Québécois, as Abdallah calls them, because they always had pretty curtains. I never understood why they moved so often. But what surprised me even more was that as soon as they moved into a new house, they settled in as if they were going to stay there for the rest of their lives. They repainted the walls, they decorated the place, and they put up new curtains. I envied them a little ... I began to think that over here curtains were a bit like flags.

Now that we have enough money to buy some curtains, now that we've gone back to live in Lebanon and have all come back to Canada again, now that we aren't moving as often as we used to, I've developed an allergy to dust ...

Salim's business was thriving. The children helped out a lot. Without Abdallah and Samira, who had quit school so they could go to work, he would never have been able to open a second store, and then a third one in a neighbouring town. Many people are surprised that immigrants who arrive with empty pockets can improve their living conditions so quickly. They forget about the contribution of their children. We were not used to paying them for their work, so we didn't pay them. I only learned much later that this wasn't done over here.

As Salim had fewer financial worries, he started treating me better. Sometimes, he would look at me as if he were seeing me for the first time. He even bought me a fur coat because I could not get used to the cold. Maybe I just didn't go out often enough.

They say that *a woman who is loved by her husband can even move the moon* ... The moon didn't have time to complete its full orbit before Salim began to get restless again. He wanted to go back to Lebanon! For a holiday, he claimed, but I knew full well that he was thinking of actually moving back home. When he returned from his travels, he reminded me of a politician just before an election, who shakes everyone's hand and makes lavish promises. He charmed us all with photos, postcards, presents, and enticing stories about sunshine, orchards, and seaside restaurants. To be honest, the photos were beautiful ...

My memories come back to me. They are always the same, as if there were only one image left for each period of my life. Years and years of life are disappearing from my memory. Or rather, they are changing into just a few images that I feel more than I see.

If I look quickly, I see only the centre of the image. The centre is always an emotion that I relive each time the image flashes through my brain. If I take my time, I can sometimes make out details that I hadn't noticed at first, details that have probably been part of my life ... There is certainly even more there ...

I would like to enlarge these images, to understand my life better before I die. Just for the pleasure of understanding. Just to know why I suffered, and why I sometimes want to leave this world.

Salim is leaving for Lebanon, while I stay here with the children. Abdallah and Samira have taken over the stores. The memory ends there. Until now, I have always seen it that way ...

If I look more closely, I see two teenagers just a little older than Véronique and Amélie are now ... Two children who manage three stores for more than two months! How could I have let him leave? Was I fully aware of the situation? Did I try to convince him to wait until the children were older? And Salim, who considered himself a good father, how could he leave everything without giving it any thought? And once he got there, how could he act like a rich man, merrily squandering the money his children had worked just as hard as he had to earn? It won't change anything, perhaps, but I would like to understand why I didn't say anything, why I just put up with it …

My past is voluminous, but only in the number of years I have lived, and my future is so fragile …

When I said, "Put me in a nursing home," I didn't say everything that was on my mind, but rather what I thought would be acceptable to my children. I put myself in their position, forgetting my own. That's what I always do. I didn't want them to feel that their mother might become a greater burden than she already was.

I've always needed my husband and my children to carry out the smallest tasks outside the home: going to the doctor, dentist, or hairdresser, buying the slightest piece of clothing, paying a bill, calling the plumber, or reading a letter. I can't do anything by myself. One day, I dialed 911, and when I gave my address, they didn't understand me … I don't know how to do anything on my own.

Most of the time, my husband and children take care of everything. I don't even have to pester them. But I don't think it's normal.

This kind of dependence, even though I'm quite used to it, is still difficult for me. The day my body lets me down and prevents me from doing my work around the house, how will I stand it? If I become more dependent than I already am, it will be unbearable. How can I resign myself to being useless one day? Completely useless. I cannot.

I understand why so many old people lose their minds.

I pretend to be a wise woman who is unphased by anything, who is calmly letting go of life … And to think that some people believe me …

Samir breezed in to pick me up so I could go babysit for Julien and Gabriel. Predictably, he forgot to bring me what I had asked for—empty glass jars and plastic containers. They always have too many of them, and as I never buy prepared food, I don't have the containers I need to send food for the children. But I'll have all the time in the world to fill up many bagsful this evening while waiting for them to come home.

When Amélie isn't able to look after her little brothers, and they can't find a babysitter, either Samir or his wife Jacinthe comes to get me at the last minute. Grandmothers are made for times like this—they're always available. It's nice for everyone. But if they gave me a little more time to get ready, it would be even better.

Gabriel was already asleep, and Julien wanted to do arts and crafts. I had to open all the drawers and cupboards to find a pair of scissors. My God, what a lot of stuff! It takes me by surprise every time. I think that I'll never get used to the sheer quantity of objects and products that pile up in people's homes. And just think of everything that gets thrown out. The number of rolls of scotch tape of all sizes, and tubes of glue—glue for plastic, wood, and paper, glue for this and glue for that—which just end up drying out in a drawer. And it's the same for everything else. Lovely paper bags, plastic bags, glass jars, and plastic containers that would have delighted the villagers back home. We only had containers made of clay or wicker, which we used and reused. Here, there are so many sprays, bottles, creams, and cotton balls for the eyes, skin, and ears. And so much paper that gets thrown out after hardly being used. Powdered and liquid soap—one kind to be used on floors, another for toilet or sinks, one kind for washing clothes in cold water, another for washing them in hot water. Blue liquid for washing windows, another product for stove-tops, and yet another kind of cleaning agent for the inside of the oven. One disinfectant for this, another for that. The number of discs, cassettes, and video tapes they record and then never listen to or watch because there are always new movies to watch. Cupboards and chests are overflowing with games, toys, and gadgets. When they were little, Samir and Myriam's children used to play with pots and pans and cardboard boxes ...

So many objects! What could they all be for? Why do we need so many things? I just can't understand why anyone would need all that. Here, houses have as much space for storage as they do for living. Even I have a machine to wash the dishes; I have one machine to wash clothes, one to dry the clothes, and another to clean the floors. I have a machine for grinding chickpeas, another for grinding meat, and yet another for making juice. Why? Am I happier or less tired? They've invented all these machines for our comfort. But you pay a price for comfort: you work harder and then you are more tired. There's no going back because people are used to what they have. And everyone does what the others are doing ... *If you want to live among the blind, you have to be prepared to lose an eye yourself* ...

Of all the things people have invented, supposedly to make our lives easier, I find the telephone the most extraordinary. Since the rise of big cities, it's been the nicest invention ...

We didn't find any scissors, which would have been useful. So, Julien took out his coloured pencils—he has tons of them—and started drawing. He draws well, like his uncle Farid.

When I have a pencil in my hand, I draw a bird. It's always the same bird, which I like to draw perched on a branch. I also know how to draw rabbits, but I don't find them as beautiful as birds. Two or three years ago, Myriam's kids were at our house. David was drawing and Véronique was reading. I don't know exactly how it happened, but that day Véronique taught me how to write my name. Since then, I write my name whenever I have a pencil in my hand.

"What does Dounia mean?" Véronique asked me, as she held my hand and helped me draw the letters. I understood the question, but I didn't know how to answer her. Abdallah, who was at the house that day, answered for me. I saw the surprise on Véronique's face when she said, "The universe? Really? That's a funny name!" Then, after thinking about it, with the same expression as her mother, she added, "But I feel that the name suits you perfectly, as if it was made for you." Abdallah translated what she'd said.

Birds are what I draw best. I draw families of birds. I can tell that they aren't all the same—one might have a smaller eye, the other a bigger head. Sheets and sheets of paper filled with bird families. I don't like to have a solitary bird sitting on a large leaf with a lot of white space around it. So, I keep on going. I give him a brother, a sister …

The last time I found myself all alone in a blank space was when my brother Musa had just died. The news came by telephone. I screamed and cried, but no one came. Musa was the only brother I'd really gotten to know. The others had all emigrated to Argentina when I was little. Musa was the one who'd helped me when I needed it. He's gone. Dead. I'll never see him again. Thirty years without seeing him, and

I'd still held out hope. If I hadn't received that phone call, I would have kept on hoping.

Does a bird shed tears like we do? Salim wasn't at home that evening. At the time, he was coming and going constantly: from Montreal to Beirut and his village Bir Barra, and then back to Montreal. He was looking for a place to settle down, a place where he'd feel content. When he was here, he missed his country; when he was there, he missed his children. I was alone that evening. I hung up the telephone, and the space around me grew so big.

My children are usually there for me when I need something. They've been helping me since they were little, God bless them. An uneducated mother is a heavy burden for her children, especially when she's isolated by the foreign language she speaks. I don't know what happened that evening. They were busy, away somewhere—I don't remember. No one. Or perhaps they didn't realize how important that piece of news was. Or perhaps I didn't even call them. Maybe I couldn't remember any of their phone numbers. I didn't know anything anymore. When you suffer too much, you can go crazy. And yet, I should have been used to it …

Each form of suffering is different. Each time, it affects a different part of your body. When your brother dies, your whole body collapses, melts away, you feel pain everywhere and nowhere … The death of a child … No.

Does a bird fall out of its nest when its brother dies? When a chick falls from the tree and dies, does the mother bird die too?

Can you ever get used to death?

Please, God, let me die before my children.

Julien wanted me to tell him a bedtime story. I told him I would sing him a song that I used to sing to his father when he was little. That made him very happy. He jumped into bed, closed his eyes, and waited for me to riffle through my memory to find the song. He was already asleep before the end …

Samir hardly ever talks to his children. It doesn't matter very much to his children whether he's at home or travelling—he's always busy or worried about something. I told him, "Your children are a treasure, my son, your only treasure."

"You're right, Mother," he replied, leaving for work without even glancing at Amélie, who was sick that day. Luckily, his wife takes good care of her kids. But she also works outside the home and is always in a rush like him. I don't know how today's women do it. I get exhausted just watching them ...

When I think about Samir and his children, I am reminded of the story about the man and his horse. Maybe I should tell him the story, rather than telling him, over and over, "Your children are your only treasure," which has never changed anything.

Every day, after washing, grooming, and feeding his magnificent horse, the man would sit down nearby and take a long look at the horse. One day, for reasons I'm unaware of, the man had to go away for a month or two and had to hire someone to take care of the horse. He showed the caretaker what to do and left more than enough oats and other grains for the horse to eat. Then he left. When he returned, the horse was skin and bones, his coat was lacklustre, and he looked nothing like the magnificent beast he once was. At first, the man thought that the caretaker had sold the oats instead of feeding them to the horse. The caretaker flatly denied this, adamantly stating that he had fed the horse properly every day. The two men went to see a judge, who asked each of them to describe, in detail, a day in the life of the horse.

The only difference the judge noticed was the man's caring gaze and the loving attention he gave his horse. He came to the following conclusion: the caretaker had not stolen the oats, he had indeed fed and groomed the horse, as he had been instructed to do, but he hadn't looked at it ... That was the only thing missing, the only one, but it was enough to make the horse gradually languish ...

Unlike Samir, Myriam only has eyes for her children—and her computer. When I see her chatting with her daughter, her son, or the two of them at the same time, I try not to make any noise and to fade into the background. They forget about me very quickly. I catch a few words here and there, but not the full meaning of what they are saying. I hang on to their smiles and laughter, which I feel deep down inside. I am happy and nostalgic, but at the same time, sorry about the life I never had and would have so much liked to live.

I remember what I was like, as a motherless child, and I see my children, who are also motherless. My mother and I spoke the same language, but soon she was no longer there to talk to me. When I became a mother, I wasn't there for my children either. I fed them, that's all. I didn't speak to them; we never talked to each other. I've missed out on something that will forever be beyond my reach. When I got out of my prison, it was too late—my children were already grown. I know that language was a barrier, but so was misfortune. Misfortune is an insurmountable wall, a prison with all its doors slammed shut, held in place with multiple locks. You must serve your time. Then, one day, the doors swing open and you are freed. But during your prison term, you try to stay alive, just in case you get out one day. Yet, you're sure it's forever. So, what I wonder today is why we go on living when we know full well that our misfortune will last forever?

It's possible that my memory of those days is darker than what I actually lived through. Perhaps hope and despair are intertwined, and we experience them one after the other or else both at the same time ... Misfortune kept me isolated from life, and in that isolation, I found the strength to keep on living ...

Samir and his wife rarely come home when they've said they will. It doesn't matter, as long as they're having a good time. It's strange how the hours I spend waiting for them are different from the hours I spend at my own house. I'm home alone very often and the evenings seem to go by in a flash. I never look at the clock …

When I was about twelve years old, I was as skinny as a rail and as brown as a berry, but in those days, I had no complexes, as educated people would say now. One day, I asked my father, "Which of your children do you love the most?"

He answered, "I love the littlest ones until they grow up, the sickest ones until they get better, and the farthest ones until they come home again."

"And me? I'm not little, I'm not sick, and I'm right here beside you."

"The little ones grow up, the sick ones eventually get better, and the farthest ones come home, but you're always my child, until death, even beyond death."

He stroked my hair, and a shiver ran down my spine. It was very rare for him to touch me. I think that he never even kissed me. I would kiss his hand, sometimes, like those who came to visit him did. But I knew he loved me. I knew it.

The other day, Amélie asked her father the same question. He looked at her with a strange expression on his face, surprised by the question. He did love her, he replied.

"You love Julien and Gabriel more than me," said Amélie.

"You are my child, Julien and Gabriel are my children, I love all three of you the same."

I understood everything. *Love, child, more, same, three*— all simple words. Amélie didn't look satisfied with her father's answer.

None of my children had ever asked me that kind of question. Maybe they did and without thinking, I might have answered, "I don't know, go ask your father." But I think I'd remember, because I remember the day I asked my father that very question myself … I would have been just as surprised as Samir and would have given the same answer as he did, "I love all my children the same." But now that I have time to think about it, now that there's no one standing in front of me waiting for me to answer—and it's me, instead, who's waiting for Samir who isn't coming home anytime soon—I would add that I'm happy with those who are happy and unhappy with those who are not. My heart and soul are divided into six pieces—no, not pieces but rather branches. I have a heart with six branches, and if you added my grandchildren, that would make eleven branches.

With Abdallah, I learn about courage, with Samira, I learn about order, with Farid, I learn about silence, with Samir, I learn how to think about myself, with Myriam, I learn to think, with Kaokab, I learn to laugh, with Véronique, I learn about intelligence, with David, I learn about love, with Amélie, I learn about hope, with Julien, I learn to play, and with Gabriel, I learn how to live.

And what do I teach my children? I love them, that's all. I wish I could spare them suffering, at least. That my own suffering could help them, at least.

Don't teach your child anything, destiny will take care of that ...

I lived through what I had to, and they will live through what they have to. That's the way it is.

But what purpose does it serve to have come into the world before them? That's what I'll never understand ...

I wish that someone had warned me about life ...

When I was a very young girl, my brother and I would often go with the shepherd who led our goats to a neighbouring mountain. That's perhaps where I get my need to see things from afar and my fondness for peace and quiet. Seeing my village become a tiny speck in the distance taught me one thing: seen from up above, all the sons and daughters of Adam are very small indeed. Even Munir Effendi, who fancied himself a pasha, with clothes that were always clean and a neatly waxed moustache, who sported a tarboosh, and who went around kicking poor people and showing disdain for them—even he was a mere mortal, and just as small as other people.

Around the same time, my father would sometimes put food into baskets and ask us to deliver them to different houses, to the Druze or Christians—it didn't matter—but we had to make sure that no one saw us. My brother and I were proud to carry out this task without being seen, although we didn't know why we had to do so in secret. Much later, when I asked him why, my father explained. His words still give me pause, even now.

"Everyone thinks that the poor need the rich, but it's the other way around. I'm not rich, I live off what the earth and animals provide, and what my sons send me from Argentina. But I have enough to give a little bit of help to those in need. If these people knew that it came from me, they would come to thank me, whereas I'm the one who's grateful to them, for they enable me to fulfill my duty," said my father.

"It's more difficult to receive than to give," he continued. "In giving there's a hint of vanity while receiving requires great dignity. Being poor in our society and not feeling humiliated demands great strength of character. It's a great test. There's no need to add to it." He then started looking out over the village. We were on the front balcony, which allowed us to see nearly all the houses. There were about a hundred of them, half of which were inhabited by his parishioners.

"There isn't one single house that wasn't built or rebuilt without money sent by expats. Our country is the envy of many people. Yet, in order to survive, we who live here rely on help from other countries like Brazil, Argentina, Canada, and the United States. But if you think about it, they also need us because if all immigrants stayed in their homelands there wouldn't be enough workers in all those vast and sparsely populated countries. You see, the mouse needs the lion just as much as the lion needs the teeth of the little mouse … *Everything, even the smallest pebble, has its purpose and can help to prop up the jug* … and if the jug is not stable, it's difficult to pour out the water it contains. As the Hindus say, 'Everything is connected, and each living creature has its place and its own importance.'" My father often spoke to us about Gandhi, whom he admired greatly.

Apart from Abdallah, my children remember very little about their grandfather. What a pity.

I've always known that it's harder to receive than to give, but I never knew how much harder. Where does dignity come from? My father spoke like this when he was still in good health. I would have liked to hear him talk about the dignity of receiving toward the end of his life. It's true that men are more accustomed to receiving and being served.

When I was little, I didn't think I would become a grand-mother—a mother, yes, but not a grandmother. When I looked at my own grandmother, I found her so old. I used to tell myself that I wouldn't like to live that long. I didn't think that I'd get to that stage so quickly ... Still, having grandchildren is the only good thing about getting old ... For everything else, you have to rationalize—that's life, you can't do anything about it, it happens to everyone, if you're alive, you can't help getting old ... and dying ... But how can you remain reasonable when you can't stop your nose from running and your bladder from leaking ...

One day, my children will feed me as I once fed them, and they'll change my diapers, too ... Receiving requires dignity ... Oh my God, please let me die before I get to that stage!

I came to Canada by boat with five children, and about fifteen years later I returned to Lebanon by boat with four children. The ship was pretty much the same, but not the journey. It was marvellous. A dream voyage that lasted eighteen days and eighteen nights. My children had grown up, they knew how to read and write, and they spoke two or three languages. We had money. Samira had a good time taking care of everything, while Samir, Myriam, and Kaokab had a good time doing nothing. I wasn't used to having no worries and doing nothing. Food was placed on the table. All we had to do was eat, stroll around, rest, watch movies, and gaze at the sea and the sky.

I was worried about landing in Lebanon, though. I tried not to think about it, and to enjoy my vacation to the fullest, as those who are used to vacationing would say. To be honest, I didn't really want to live in Lebanon. I'd just become used to living in Canada, and I wasn't eager to change. If my father, my brothers, and my sister had still been in Lebanon, things would have been different, but they'd all gone to Argentina. And I had no lady friends there. Salim had managed to sell us on his dream. But since my children wanted to go live in paradise, I said to myself, I'm going to go there, too. I would even have followed them to live in hell!

Salim's cousins were expecting us. They knew about our plans, and we were going to stay with them until we rented an apartment. I recalled the time when we lived with Monsieur and Madame Archambault, and I got the shivers thinking about the cousins, who had a small apartment in a noisy neighbourhood of Beirut.

Abdallah had stayed behind to help his father wind up his business. Farid didn't come either, thinking fewer children would ease the burden on me, although he mostly just wanted to get away from his brother Samir.

I don't often think back to those years, when my sons Farid and Samir turned into thieves, liars, and rebels—strangers who no longer spoke our language. Hatred had seeped into their adolescent hearts, and we didn't know how to reach them or talk sense into them. After going from one reform school to another, they were headed straight for adult prisons. I spent so many nights waiting for them, and so many hours trying to figure out how to avoid trouble when they did come home. Salim grew more and more violent toward them, and they got more and more out of control. I was so afraid.

By separating them, we were hoping to put them back on track.

We were at our wits' end, powerless. We felt as though we were about to lose them forever. I was nostalgic for the time when all I had to do was feed them. Now, my sons needed more, but I didn't know what. Salim blamed the company they kept, the influence of gangs of youngsters who had dropped out of school. But I knew that the fault also lay in what was happening at home. The values that we were trying to pass on to them, sometimes forcibly, seemed ridiculous to them. Everything beyond the home attracted them more than anything we had to offer. Salim tended to embellish everything, to glorify our culture, our customs, and our ancestors, thereby disparaging the culture here. That widened the gap between us. Maybe I was to blame, too, without realizing it.

Farid and Samir were not sitting in two chairs like Abdallah and Samira, but rather standing on the top rail of a chairback about to topple over in the middle of the street. It was as if they no longer had any roots. Outside the home, they were regarded as foreigners, the "Syrian brothers," as the kids their age would call them. At home, they felt like foreigners, too. But, when all was said and done, they preferred to be foreigners outside the home than to be foreigners with us. Bit by bit, they slipped through our fingers.

What they had left was the bond they shared with each other. United in adversity, supporting each other, one of them would take a beating to prevent the other from being beaten up. It hurt me to separate them because I knew what it meant to be alone, but we had to do it. We were not wrong. Samir went back to school in Lebanon. He got married a few years later and had three children. Farid never liked school, never had kids, but he didn't end up in jail. He held on to a deep-seated rebelliousness from that time. Sometimes, I look at him, surreptitiously, and I recall all the years when I was so afraid of losing him. I didn't lose him, but I haven't completely got him back either.

Beirut! Salim should never have told us about it. The port of Beirut in July was like hell on earth. After the tranquillity of the ship and the beauty of the ocean, we were overwhelmed by the heat, humidity, and stench. We were suffocating. I had never seen so many people or heard so much noise in such a small and filthy space. My children wanted to get back on the boat and return to Canada. Me, too. But as their mother, I told them to be patient, that we would get out of it alive, and that things would be better when we went to live with our cousins. But it wasn't any better at the cousins' place. Their apartment was even smaller than I'd imagined. It was packed to the rafters with people who'd come to welcome us, when all we needed was a bit of fresh air so we could breathe ...

When we arrived in Beirut, we had to fall in line at once. Some things were done, and others were not. There was a way of behaving when you were with other people and there were rules of decorum. You had to know what to hide and what you were able to reveal, what was forbidden and what was permitted. With time, I'd forgotten all these rules. Sometimes, I felt like my children, rebelling against all the endless ceremonial customs, against the rules and regulations that no longer made sense to us. But as a mother, I needed to set an example and I did so, somewhat grudgingly, trying my best to hide my true feelings.

Had I changed so much or had I always been allergic to decorum? To my surprise, I felt so foreign.

Though language was no longer a barrier for me, I quickly realized that I didn't have an affinity for people who spoke my language. Except for the childhood friends I had lost—one had moved away and the other had died—I hadn't formed any real friendships in either of the two countries I'd lived in for such a long time. There was no one I could have called "my friend," which is what Salim and the children called the people they hung out with. Perhaps Salim is right: I am an outsider, a "barbarian," as the Greeks used to call foreigners. He's absolutely right. I've been a barbarian for so long that I've grown accustomed to it ... and I like it.

There were still advantages to living in Beirut. I could do my shopping alone. I didn't need to go very far at all. A grocery store, a butcher shop, and a bakery were located on the ground floor of our apartment building. The merchants understood me, even though, in their eyes, my mountain accent, my western clothing, and the fact that I spoke neither French nor English didn't go together.

In Lebanon, we were called "Americans" whereas in Canada, in the early years, we were called "Syrians." In my husband's village, they used the name of my village when referring to me. When I think about it, I haven't been called Dounia since I left the village where I was born …

The second advantage was radio and television. I could follow the news without always having to ask Salim or Abdallah what was happening in the world. I no longer had to guess the plots of the American shows I'd watched in Canada. I understood them. When I watched comedies produced in Lebanon, I even laughed along with other people.

The neighbours were another advantage, although sometimes a drawback as well. During the fifteen years I'd lived in Canada, and even in the time since we'd been back in Lebanon, I'd never gone to have coffee at a neighbour's house. It's a small thing, but a pleasant one, and it helps the time go by. On the other hand, neighbours who sit around for hours, who want to know everything, who gossip about you, and exaggerate or twist what you tell them, who even say bad things about people behind their backs while flattering and praising them to their faces … soon enough, they tend to turn on the "Americans."

Beirut! When I was young, proper glue wasn't readily available the way it is today. So, some people would use crushed raisins to stick things together, but only for the sake of appearances. Because, of course, things fell apart again after a while. After years of living in Canada, Beirut made me think of a city held together with raisins. I was surprised to see the difference between the front and back of buildings, as if they weren't the same structures. The facades were stylish while the back of the buildings looked decrepit and dirty, with cracked or crumbling walls. It was long before the war, in the years when the banks were filling their coffers with oil money from other Arab countries, when the rich were growing richer while the poor got poorer. During those years, the nouveau riche multiplied like locusts and strutted around as if they had forgotten that *their father's tarboosh was still hanging from the branch of a mulberry tree.* They flaunted their newly acquired wealth, their facades, unaware that their behind was still showing. For Beirut of the day, and maybe Beirut today, will fifteen years of war be enough to change mentalities? Appearances were all that mattered.

I come from the mountains. I was raised differently. I am never misled by appearances. As my father often said, "*Greet strangers in keeping with their clothing, but bid them farewell in keeping with their intelligence.*" Appearances never matter for long.

We all struggled to adapt to our new life and new country. Even Salim, who had dreamed so big and who had made us dream along with him. The only things that lived up to their promise were the weather and the beauty of the mountains. There were cozy restaurants on the waterfront, it's true, and you could ski in the mountains and swim in the ocean on the same day, but by the time we figured out where and how to do it, we had run out of money.

The people of Beirut are true merchants. In a country where there is no safety net or government support, where you go to the hospital with a severed leg in one hand and a fistful of money in the other, or else you stay outside on the street, the survival of the fittest is key. The "fittest" is often the one who lies the best and who manages to cheat those who don't lie as skilfully. Not to mention those who are addicted to money, and who need more and more of it. Lying comes naturally, and when they speak, they do so to charm and deceive others. That's the way it is. Salim was reluctant to admit it until he was completely fleeced himself. He, too, comes from the mountains. He is naïve, honest— even too honest. He trusts other people and thinks they are like him. In Canada, he was successful because of those qualities, because honesty was the norm back then. I don't know if it's still the same these days, because the country has suffered economic hardships.

I often told him, "*Close the door and trust your neighbour.*" But what good does talking do if no one is listening? In the blink of an eye, we were just as poor as we had been during the early years in Canada. The grinding poverty we were experiencing was even more bitter because we had grown accustomed to a certain level of comfort, particularly because we had lived an isolated life in Canada, where we were the sole judges and witnesses of our wealth or poverty, our happiness or misery. In Beirut you couldn't burrow yourself in your home; you lived under the constant gaze of your neighbours. Like it or not, it was difficult to escape. Beirut had all the drawbacks of a small town or even village with the pretensions of a big city. Everything revolved around appearances, superficiality, and glitz. Here it's the complete opposite. Québécois are modest—sometimes even self-deprecating—which is not necessarily better. Whereas the Lebanese crow about their so-called superiority, bragging and even taking credit for things they haven't done, Québécois brood over their so-called inferiority, don't draw sufficient attention to their accomplishments, and even forget what they've done. No one has an accurate perception of their own worth …

As I sit here in my rocking chair, I tend to brood more than I crow. If I had to stand up and say what I think out loud, I would be speechless, or I would perhaps utter a few halting words. If I ever stopped dwelling on the past, I might start being who I am and I wouldn't be afraid of speaking anymore.

I dig and dig in the remains of my memory, hoping to one day find peace in this head full of holes and crevices.

I remember a Christmas Eve without snow when we didn't have a cent to our name. My children, the ones who were working, hadn't received a paycheck. Salim, who was once again penniless, had gone back to live in his village. We were resigned to spending a rather dreary Christmas Eve, like the ones in the black-and-white movies sometimes shown on television around Christmas. But just like in those films, right before the end, a miracle happened. My daughter Samira found a bill worth one hundred Lebanese pounds that she had squirreled away and forgotten about. It was enough to pay for a feast! I remember that we all began to dance for joy. For a few moments, we felt like the richest people on earth.

Poverty is always hard, but when combined with spiritual misery, it becomes inhumane. I will never forget the day when we had to take my son Abdallah to the hospital because he had taken too much of his medication. We had no money. I looked in all the drawers but found nothing. There wasn't a penny for the taxi or for the hospital ... Oh, my God, why do I dwell on the past? Why do I relive my gut-wrenching pain as if it were just yesterday?

It's over ... The sorrow is subsiding ... I wish that someday I could think about those times without pain. I need a miracle, just like in those old black-and-white movies.

Eventually, my children began to leave for other countries, practically fleeing as soon as they had saved a bit of money. Not one of them managed to adapt, to put down roots ... They say that *raising a child is more critical than nursing one*. You can't turn back the clock. When you leave your village or your country, you leave for life. At one point, one of my children lived in Brazil, another in France, the third in Canada, the fourth in Indonesia, and the rest of the family in Lebanon.

Then the war broke out. We were expecting it. What we had once called the Lebanese miracle was no more. We knew that something serious was going to happen, but no one had imagined its scale; no one could have predicted that it would last for more than fifteen years. Chaos soon took hold. Salim and Abdallah read as many newspapers as they could, but still didn't understand. It didn't take long before no one understood what was happening over our heads. The war forced everyone to revert to their original clan. At the same time, alliances between clans and countries were being formed, dissolved, and remade at a dizzying pace.

So many men convinced others to follow them and play at making war against one another. There was nothing you could do but keep quiet and wait until they burned themselves out. How many thousands of people lost their lives in these senseless and self-centred games. There was nothing you could do but scream and weep. They fired point blank at women, who gathered from all communities to march resolutely for peace. And there was nothing you could do but wish that you could crawl back into your mother's womb and wait for better days to come. Each of the warring factions believed they wielded power whereas power was actually in the hands of stupidity and vanity, on all sides, inside and outside the country. All you could do was laugh.

The war forced people who had enough money to flee, go into exile, and leave behind members of their family who were just barely covered with fresh earth. I can hardly bring myself to picture mothers and fathers looking out of an airplane window for one last glimpse of the land where the life of their child had been snatched from them.

Thousands of families were scattered across the globe as a result of the war. For us, thank God, it was the opposite: war brought us all together again. Gradually, we were all reunited in the country where my children had grown up.

I grabbed my coat and left as quickly as I could. Usually, Myriam comes with me. She either drives me home or walks with me. I didn't wait for her this time. Luckily, I didn't have to put on my boots. If I had, she would have had time to catch up with me.

Since we started working together, as she calls it, it's been as regimented as in the army. Twice a week—on Mondays and Thursdays—I get to her place by ten o'clock in the morning and stay until five in the afternoon. She wanted me to go over four times a week! I've always had trouble saying no, but this time it just popped out of my mouth, effortlessly, and she didn't insist. She often invites me to stay for supper. When the children are there, I'm more easily persuaded to stay.

The day Myriam told me that she wanted to write a book about me, I laughed. But I confess that I was a bit flattered, and surprised, too. Then she asked me what I thought about it.

"Since when have you asked for my opinion about a book you're going to write?" I replied, or something like that. The little rascal! As I now know, she needed me.

I'd forgotten how charming she can be when she wants to. She managed to convince me, the little devil!

At first, I found it fun. It was the first time I'd worked outside the home. Of course, my daughter was not paying me, but it's normal in families not to pay for services rendered. My salary was the pleasure I got and gave to my daughter. In a way, I was involved in her profession. For me, that was important, and I was proud of it. For the first time in my life, someone needed me for something other than what I knew how to make. For the first time, someone needed to know what I was thinking, what I wanted in life, what I'd been, and what I'd become. I was at the centre of a body of knowledge no one else possessed but me.

By means of coffee and wine, questions and patience, Myriam helped me unravel the threads of my life. I was nervous at first, but Myriam was good at putting me at ease. I recounted incidents that I remembered. I gradually began to enjoy myself. When I wasn't with her, I was thinking about the stories I would tell her. I didn't watch television in the evening anymore. Instead, I thought about my life, and gathered the fragments of my past.

Myriam is very curious … she *needs to know who laid the egg and who built the chicken coop* … Everything was going smoothly until one day when she became very demanding. Increasingly demanding. She wanted to know what I didn't know, and she wanted me to remember what I'd forgotten.

Sometimes, she wanted me to think like her, to tell her what she wanted to hear. She put words in my mouth.

I don't understand why she wanted to know the truth about me, why she wanted to dig further, deeper, always closer to the heart. At the same time, it seemed like she wanted to masquerade the truth, change it, or make it more dramatic.

And then, there are things I don't want to talk about. That's why I left just now. I'm willing to help her, but not become her slave! It's her book, not mine.

Myriam would suck my blood to write her book. I'm exaggerating a little because I'm tired, but that's almost the truth. It's not that she's mean. She's just very strong-willed. All that matters to her is finishing what she's started. Let her do it by herself—I'm fed up now. I've already seen her get up at four in the morning to write. The sun wasn't even up yet and there she was, already seated at her desk with her coffee and cigarettes and her piles of books and papers. I've told her a hundred times that she shouldn't smoke before breakfast, that it's bad for her health. She doesn't give a damn. The only thing she cares about is finishing the book she's writing. And when she finishes one, she immediately starts another, which she absolutely has to finish. As if there weren't enough books in the world already!

I'd been talking for weeks. I'm not a watermelon, which is nourishing and thirst-quenching, but also good fodder for donkeys.

"Maybe you aren't tired of listening to me, but I'm tired of talking. I'm old, you forget that sometimes. I'm not as healthy as I used to be," I told her.

She didn't want to understand. She began to ask her questions all over again. Then, I uttered a proverb she hates, *"Those who are born are entrapped, whereas those who die are at rest."* Myriam doesn't want to believe that we are each a toy in the hands of fate, that we don't always have a choice, that life is sometimes a burden, and that death can be a deliverance.

She repeated what I'd just said, and added, "Yes, but … you could have … if you had wanted to." I realized, then, that she wasn't able to put herself in my shoes.

Her face changed, just as I expected. She was about to move on to another question when I said,

"Whether you like it or not, this proverb defines my life. If you want to write about me, you can't gloss over it and pretend that it hasn't been part of your daily life, too."

Then she tried to calm me down by saying that I was the best mother ever, that no one else could have done better than me. I was beside myself. Although I am usually calm, this time I burst out,

"Are you writing this book to cover things up, to sweep them under the rug as I've done my whole life, or else to show the true face of your mother? Please don't tell me that I helped you understand life the way a mother should. You have seen me remain submissive, compliant, and silent. Is this the kind of life my daughters should emulate? You can't bring children into this world and then just let them fend for themselves. A caged animal—that's the kind of mother you've had! I've never done anything worthwhile for you or any of my children because I couldn't see anything from the cage I was locked up in. Ignorant—that's what I've been. It's been a disaster. I've lived in darkness and given nothing to my children. You've been like orphans, without a father or mother. You would have been better off if you had been true orphans. It would have been better for me, as well, because all my love has not changed anything.

"What is done is done. No words will take me back to the age of five, before my mother died. No words will give you another mother or another father. No words will give us a different past. Those who are born are entrapped, whereas those who die are at rest. That is my truth."

Although I'm generally mute, I'm capable of speaking when I take pains to do so or when the pain becomes too great and overflows.

Once Myriam's kids came home for lunch, the atmosphere changed. That's just how I am. A little smile, and black can turn into white. Before he went back to school, David asked, "Are you sad, *Sitto*?"

"No, not sad," I replied, "just old, that's why." He didn't look convinced, though.

Myriam made coffee, and I tried to delay the moment when she would start to ask questions again. I talked about the weather, as people who live in cold climates tend to do. I talked about the delicious grapes she had put out on the table, about Salim, who's said he would like to see her from time to time, about Abdallah who was doing well, but who missed her ever since she told him not to come over to her place … Just as *money begets money and lice bring on nits*, one word leads to another.

"Me? ... The most important? ... My children ... The most important thing in my life? It's ... wait ... let me think about it ... I would say it's emigrating. Yes. Changing countries. Because that completely changed my life and the lives of my children. But, when I think about it a little longer, I realize that no, that's not what changed my life ... It's ..."

I knew where she was going.

"I beg of you," I shouted. "I don't want you to talk about Abdallah in your book. Especially not if you're quoting me. Please don't put me in that story. He is my son—may God keep your children in good health—he is my son, and anything I could say about him would fall far short of the truth. Anything I could say would be so far from what I have lived through that I prefer not to talk about it at all. Please understand, he is my first born, the first child to have drunk milk from my breast, to have been nourished by my body. He is the one I have loved above all else. He is my flesh and blood. What did I do? What didn't I do? Was it because we left our country? Were his roots too deeply entrenched there, or perhaps he never put roots down anywhere? Even over there, he was different from the others. I gave him too many responsibilities when his father left for America. It was his destiny. My destiny. It's what God handed me and made me endure—to teach me something, to punish me. What did I do? I wish I'd learned my lesson some other way. I wish I'd been punished another way. I've told you a hundred times that I didn't want to talk about it. And I don't want to talk about it now!"

I ran away. That was the right thing to do. That will teach her a thing or two. I can't just cut my heart out and place it on her desk so she can write about it ... She'd have to feel it in her own gut to understand me.

Abdallah is her brother, not her child!

I know that she, too, has felt the burden of Abdallah's illness. The entire family has been distressed, but nothing can be worse than suffering from your own child's suffering.

It's almost spring ...

Perhaps I could go the long way around and walk past the school my grandkids go to. My little darlings ... Amélie, Véronique, and David ... No, they would be embarrassed if they saw me. I could just watch them from afar, and then they wouldn't notice me ... At their age, I remember, I didn't really like my grandmother to come to the village square when I was there with my girlfriends. When you are young, you think of your grandparents as frozen in one place and you don't want to see them anywhere else. Then one day, you come back to the place where you always saw them, and they're no longer there ... That's life ...

I hope it won't start snowing again. It's so nice to walk around without boots. They haven't put the benches back along the sidewalks yet. I would have liked to sit down for a while, to rest and watch the children coming out of school. I could go sit down in a café, order a cappuccino, and drink it slowly while looking out the window. But I've never gone into a coffee shop, a movie theatre, or a store by myself. Except for the corner grocery store near our house and the store that's close to Myriam's place. Can you still change your habits when you're my age? What's stopping me? I have enough money to pay for what I need, so what's the problem? When I told Myriam that fear made the world go 'round, I was surely referring to my own fear.

I remember going to my daughters' school one day when they were handing out their year-end report cards. Samira had come first in her class, and Myriam second. I think I've never been as proud in my entire life.

We'd been living in Canada for about five years, and it was the first time I'd left the house alone. It was a real outing. At the time, we were living on Charbonneau Street in Terrebonne, and my daughters' school wasn't far from home. It was about halfway between our house and Salim's store.

I dressed my youngest daughter, who must have been nearly four years old. I put on my prettiest dress, a green one with pink and red flowers. And I walked there. The more I walked, the more I blushed. Not from shame—far from it. I could hold my head high because I knew my daughters were doing well in school. I was blushing out of fear, fear that someone would stop me in the street and ask me a question. I was afraid of revealing that I didn't know how to speak, and that I came from someplace else.

I now know that it wouldn't have mattered, that no one would have insulted me or laughed at me, that my little girl would have been able to speak for me because she spoke French very well. But as I walked alone with my young daughter, who already spoke better than I did, I suddenly felt totally disconnected from everything around me. I felt that without my husband and children, I was naked, completely naked. At home, I was protected by the four walls, by the roof, by all the work I had to do, and by Salim, who spoke the same language as I did. At home, I had a reason for being. Outside, I meant nothing.

I can't remember the school ceremony very well. All the girls wore the same school uniform and, when their name was read out, each of them stepped up to collect her report card. Everyone knew the names of my daughters and knew that I was their mother.

They say that *it's impossible to hide when you're in love, pregnant, or riding a camel* ... With experience, I would add, when you're a foreigner. People stare at foreigners, no matter what they do. The more they try to blend into a crowd, the more they're noticed, like a pregnant woman trying to hide her belly.

In my husband's village, people pointed at me, commenting on my every move, even though I did my best to be discreet and act like everyone else. I know now that what I wished for wasn't realistic. It's impossible to be exactly like everyone else. Each villager was different from the others, but that bit of difference was accepted. It was part of daily life and was not noticeable. I was different in a unique way, and that was surprising to other people. When people become used to difference, it's no longer difference. The inhabitants of Terrebonne weren't used to me. How could they be? They never saw me.

I don't know if I'm right or if my old lady's mind is drifting too far from the truth …

One thing is certain. That day, no one noticed that I was shivering, that I felt completely exposed, and that I was thanking the heavens for being able to hold hands with my little girl, who was squeezing my hand very hard. Maybe they saw that my cheeks were flushed with pride. Maybe they saw that my head was held very high thanks to my daughters.

If their report cards hadn't been as good, would I have remembered this story?

Samira came over for coffee with her husband. It was a rare visit, especially on a weekday, especially because they both came, together. She wanted to tell me that they were moving to Toronto, where business was apparently better than in Montreal.

Samira is the only one in the family who married a Lebanese man. And yet, one of the reasons we went back to Lebanon was to make sure our children didn't marry strangers. My God, have I ever changed in that respect! Among our sons-in-law, daughters-in-law, boyfriends and girlfriends, or partners, as they say, Samira's husband is the only one we can speak with in our language ... But it doesn't make any difference since he does all the talking! He goes on and on about how successful he is in business and how much money he is making, as if we'd be interested in all that talk. To listen to him, you'd think that he was the one who had done it all, when everyone knows that Samira started their leather business, which was already thriving long before he came along.

Anyway ...

Samira told me that as soon as they'd settled in, she'd invite me to come spend a month with them.

"Thank you. You are very kind," I said. "We'll see what happens when the time comes." But I know that I won't go there. Sitting around waiting for her all day, not knowing what to do with my ten fingers in a house that's excessively clean and tidy, and, in the evening, listening to her husband bragging. I'd rather stay in Montreal. Myriam's husband, at least, made sure that I didn't feel out of place in their home, even though we weren't able to talk to each other. He was kind and respectful.

Samira was standing near the door. Her husband had already left.

"Mother, don't worry, we won't let you go to a nursing home," she said to me. "Actually, it's possible that we'll end up in one before you do. You're strong and in good health, you'll outlive all of us!"

You don't say things like that, even in jest. Outlive my children! Samira doesn't have children, and it shows.

After Samira left, Abdallah dropped by. He didn't even sit down. His face looked a little off ...

Myriam called me. I told her that I was sick. If she'd believed me, she would have asked me right away if I needed anything and she would have dropped in to see me.

"Are you coming over on Thursday, Mother?"

"I don't think so. Forget about all that, my love, don't keep any of what I told you. It's not worth anything. It's all lies."

"You are tired, Mother," she said. "Rest up. If you don't want to talk about Abdallah, there will be a hole. That's all. I'll fill it with something else. Don't worry about it, just rest."

And who will fill my hole, the hole I have in my heart?

I am so tired.

Not long ago, I was watching TV and saw a man lying on an operating table. His skull was open, and you could even see his brain, which looked like the beef brain I cook with garlic and lemon, except that the man wasn't dead, but just asleep. The doctor touched his brain with the tip of a needle, and the man began to speak. When the doctor removed the needle, the man stopped talking. The doctor pricked another part of the brain, and the man talked about something else. It looked as easy as lancing a blister you might get from a burn.

Does that mean that everything you experience is recorded in your brain indelibly, even if you have forgotten everything, even if you want to forget? If what I saw is true, it's both wonderful and terrifying. When you die, everything you've experienced gets erased because your brain dries out. A skeleton doesn't have any more memories. Does heredity have anything to do with the brain? Maybe not. Or with blood? The mother's blood is fertilized by the father's blood to produce a child, and their blood already contains the blood of their mothers and fathers. "Parents have eaten sour grapes and the children's teeth are set on edge," as the Bible says … My God, life is such a mystery. Is there anyone in the world who understands this, who understands everything? In the Bible, it also says, "For with much wisdom comes much sorrow, and as knowledge grows, grief increases." But is it better to die ignorant?

It would have been better if Myriam had found a way to take possession of the contents of my head, without my knowing it, along with the contents of my heart, without my having to speak.

I am so tired …

And what if Abdallah came across this book one day?

He's more nervous these days. He had an argument with his father. He doesn't come over to sit in the kitchen with me anymore, or if he does come, he leaves again very soon. Every year, I fear the worst but hope that we'll be able to avoid it.

Ever since I stopped going to Myriam's place, I've gone back to my daily routine. I rearrange the furniture, which annoys Salim. I clean the house, though he says it's clean enough. I cook, but he doesn't complain about that. If the children don't have time to come eat at our house, Salim delivers packages of food to them. He's a very efficient and willing deliveryman.

There's always something to keep me busy. When I'm finished, or even if I'm not done, I take a break to have coffee with Salim. If it's nice out, we sit on the balcony. Since Abdallah stopped having coffee at our place, since he started dropping in and leaving again suddenly, our conversations revolve around him. We've been asking ourselves the same questions for years now, and they remain unanswered. We continue to hope, that's all we can do. Will it happen again this year? What can we do to prevent it from reoccurring? How? Why?

The uphill battle has already started …

When I'm tired, when there's nothing on TV, I play solitaire. I seem to be playing a lot these days … What did I do in the past? … I must have been busy doing something before Myriam taught me how to play … to keep your mind sharp, she would say … Where are the queens? … At first, Salim thought it was boring, but he's started playing, too. That's just as well. If we're busy playing cards, we're not quarrelling. And we're not thinking about anything else either.

When I play cards with Myriam or Kaokab, we sit facing each other. We each play our own game, and we chat while we're playing. It's so much fun. If I forget to move a card, they'll point it out. My daughters have always helped me out ever since they were little. Kaokab wasn't even three years old when she did the talking—instead of me—to the milkman or the baker, who still delivered milk and bread to the house back then. My daughters have always known how to do the things that I didn't ... I have the most fun with Véronique and David, when they help me play. If Amélie is there, it's even more amusing. With the three of them around me, I'm so happy! They actually play for me. Children have such quick minds. Sometimes, they give me a little tip ... The queens are hiding ... You have to put all the cards out at the right time, or else you can't win the game ... you have to try to do your best with the hand you are dealt. It's like life. You can do your best, but you can't completely change the way things unfold ... you either have the cards or you don't. You have to make do with what you have in your hand, without cheating, because it won't help ... Oh, look ... the queens are showing their faces ... I'm afraid it may be a little late.

I haven't looked at things the same way since Myriam asked me to tell her the story of my life. I feel like I now have a better sense of what I've done with what I had. A spider who weaves her web doesn't see the web, but maybe the spider doesn't have a daughter to ask questions and make her think about her life and about life in general.

When I was young, I was strong and quick-witted, just like my granddaughter Véronique who never lets anyone walk all over her. Amélie is just the opposite. While she is still so young, a kind of silent sorrow seems to be festering within her. I don't know why, but with time, I've become weaker and weaker as I've grown older. My strength has vanished, although the love of life I've had since birth has never left me—not completely. I see that life is possible and that it can be very beautiful. At the same time, and far too often actually, I realize that I don't have the strength to make life bearable and happy …

Throughout my life I've tried to settle down, to be calm and gentle, and not to fight back. I try to lose myself in my work, to throw myself into cleaning and tidying up … But how can you maintain order in your life when everything can fall apart at any moment? All my life … no, not my whole life … since I got married, I've always tried to exercise self-control. I've tried to be patient, to take refuge in silence, telling myself that it will pass … it will pass … But it never did. The result is right here, in front of me … I've waited a long time to raise my voice. Too long. I didn't know how to do it, and my voice didn't scare anyone, only myself. It was too late … I buried my pain, I stuffed it into a jar, just like I do with zucchini, which I hollow out, salt and squeeze together so they take less space. I put a lid on the jar and seal it shut. Until next year. When my son descends into hell, it's overwhelming. It's so strong that I'm powerless, and I am dragged down like he is. I shatter into a thousand pieces and suffer senseless and excruciating pain. The packed jars rattle and crack, as if I were the only mother in the world to have a sick child.

For a while, you force yourself to forget so that you can rest a bit. The heartache fades away and gradually ebbs. Then, everything comes back unexpectedly, hits you in the face, and slams into you once again.

I am so tired …

How can I tell my daughter what I can't admit to myself?

How can I talk about fire? How can I talk about ashes?

Like me, my sons have not reached their true potential. My daughters get along fairly well in life, but I have the feeling that none of my three boys has become what he might have been. Something broke down along the way. Of course, things could always have been worse ... But something is holding them back, tearing them apart, preventing them from being ... from being happy. None of them has lost his haunted look, the look of a child who has been caught doing something wrong. Even though the two younger ones have been able to earn a good living, it feels as if everything could go off the rails at a moment's notice, as if misfortune is on the doorstep and nothing is certain. Their heads are floating somewhere, unattached to their bodies.

Maybe it was emigration that changed the course of their lives. Our arrival in Canada for the first time and then our return to Lebanon—both moves were hard on them. They say that a tree transplanted too often rarely bears any fruit you can plant. Yet, my daughters were often transplanted, as well.

Of all my children, Abdallah, the eldest, has been the least fortunate.

A long time ago, my father would tell us stories about sacrificing animals to ask for forgiveness, to give thanks to God, or for some other reason. I couldn't go along with this tradition. I didn't understand. I can understand that you might kill a goat because you need to eat. But killing it just for the sacrifice—no! Because that animal couldn't be eaten, if I remember correctly ... so it was going to die for nothing ...

No matter how much I have turned this over in my mind, I can't shake the thought of Abdallah as the sacrificial lamb of the family. They needed to find a little animal and the knife fell on him. He was slaughtered in the full flush of youth. Because he was the eldest, because he was the first born, everything fell on his shoulders. Abdallah was sacrificed. When I was a child, I didn't understand why a small animal had to suffer for all the others, and I still don't understand it.

One day, he was taken to the hospital forcibly. He came out some months later with the label "crazy" emblazoned on his forehead. The word they used was more complicated, but I prefer not to know it because it amounts to the same thing. If he had stayed in the village, if we hadn't emigrated, he would have just got into a fight with someone and been badly beaten up. He might have got up even more furious and someone else would have knocked him down again. Gradually, he would have calmed down. That's all. They wouldn't have put him in a hospital. People would have said that he had a quick temper, like his father before him, and his paternal grandfather, and his great-grandfather before that ...

Abdallah had the misfortune to spend a lot of time in hospitals. And that's the worst thing because the smell of the hospital seeps into all the pores of your body. Getting washed, wanting a new life, nothing gets done there. There are too many chemicals that make the body and mind go off the rails. It's for life. The label is sewn onto your skin. Frustration, violence, self-loathing, and shame accumulate over time and begin to spurt out from everywhere when you least expect it, when you have started to forget, thinking that it's all over and will never come back again.

Fire one day, ashes the next ... how can you talk about fire that is ignited without your knowing why and extinguished without your knowing how?

How many times have I wished that he would die—may God forgive me, how can a mother wish for her child's death, it's a betrayal of life itself—not just for my own peace, but especially for his? My child, my darling, suffering dies only with death, I know that ...

I hoped you would die, my dear child, just as I wished for my own death. Neither you nor I were meant to live in this world. As she grew older, your mother developed a shell thicker than an elephant's skin, while you, my love, are becoming weaker and weaker, less and less capable of living. I feel your fear of everything and nothing, my child, I feel your fear as if it were my own. It is my own.

Both of us have been broken, somewhere along the path of life ...

My child, for whom I first experienced the bond of motherhood, you are my first born. You are a tender child, who has been chewed up by life, chopped into tiny pieces, and sliced into slender strips of painful flesh. You, my beloved child, were still so young when you found answers to our questions and questions to our answers. Where have your beauty, your piercing eyes, and your deep gaze gone?

There have been no happy times. The days of respite have just been days of waiting, during which we slipped into a thick and dark fog. Your violence would be assuaged for a time, but it was never replaced by something alive.

Your head was heavy, and your body was nothing more than mass of flesh, barely living and laid out on a bed. For days and days, even months on end, you couldn't do more than babble. Your every breath left froth at the edge of your lips, through which the only words that passed were "let me die."

My child, what unlucky star led you to us?

My darling child, you were born to the wrong parents. Perhaps you hadn't suffered enough in a previous life or perhaps you wanted to continue the journey of mortals toward the extinction of the species. Death came to taunt you several times and continues to inflict pain again and again.

How many times have you wanted to leave this world and how many times have I held you back?

My son, the more I dwell on our lives, the more I ponder them over and over, the more I am convinced that you chose the wrong parents. It's your only mistake.

Your father wanted you to be like him. He wanted to mould you into a brave and fearless person. He wanted to make a man out of you, without understanding that you were a sensitive and gentle little boy. A man can be sensitive and gentle, too. Why do all men have to be alike? Your father wanted you to perpetuate his line of proud men given to bravado at all costs.

Our destinies were forever transformed when we were the same age. When I was eighteen, I entered a marriage, and at eighteen, you entered a hospital. We would fall, get up, fall, get up. Without reprieve. Where can you get the strength to change course?

And your sister Myriam wants me to talk about you, out loud.

What you and I have lived through is unspeakable. No book can tell the story, twenty books would never be enough. No one would understand, because even I—after living through it for all these days and nights, year after year—even I forget sometimes. My suffering subsides until the moment when everything begins to boil over again, when all the wounds reopen, and the volcano erupts. Then, everything comes back to me. Everything comes back just as violently as the first time. Only your father can understand because he is your father, because he has felt it, too, in his own gut.

If, by some misfortune, one of Myriam's children were struck by the same fate as you, she would know what I mean. She would understand without needing me to talk about it …

My God, no! God, if you have any kindness left, don't let my daughter—or any of my children—go through what I have. Suffering from your children's pain is the cruellest form of pain. Never afflict them in this way. If any of my grandchildren were to be sacrificed the way their uncle was, I would want to die right away …

There are things you cannot say, things you do not say, even to yourself, things that you would like to bury deep down inside.

And yet, there are things that bubble up to the surface, nonetheless. Like vomit, which tastes bitter and sour as you gulp it down again. There's violence that cannot be forgiven. There's violence that you would like to discount as mere madness, but it's a kind of insanity that you can never forgive, and never forget.

There are things that weigh on you, as heavy as all your fears and cowardice bound up together.

There are things that you cannot talk about, even in a whisper, because you are so ashamed of them. There is shame that never fades with time, for which you cannot forgive yourself, or forget. Shame that remains intact and always feels as razor sharp as the day you first experienced it.

I am ashamed. I have been ashamed for fifty years. Even thinking about it now, I am ashamed.

I can still hear my father's voice. I can hear it as clearly as I can see the dust-covered boot swinging toward me before striking me right in the face.

I see my father turn his back on me with contempt.

My own father and the father of my children were both on horseback, ready to leave.

"Don't go, Salim," I said, "I'm about to give birth and I don't want to be alone like I was the first two times." That's all. That's all I said to him. Was it wrong to say this to the man I'd chosen to marry, who'd chosen me to be his bride, whom no one had forced me to marry, to the man I loved? Was it wrong to ask this man to stay behind in the village while I gave birth to his third child?

It wasn't the first time that he'd hit me, but this time he dared to do it in front of my father, the most respected priest in the region, and he'd kicked me in the face, which is something you wouldn't even do to a dog.

From where he was sitting, perched high up on his horse, my father had seen everything.

My father, the person I'd considered my parent and protector, didn't react. He was expressionless. He uttered no words of sympathy, nor did he come to my defence. He didn't show this man who'd just split my lip open that I wasn't some orphan, that I had a father and a family, and that you couldn't do whatever you pleased with me.

Nothing. Not a gesture, not a word, no reproach. Nothing.

I was the one at fault. As though he were spitting in my face, he said, "A curse on those who brought you into this world!"

It was the worst insult. My own father was cursing me in front of the man who'd just humiliated me. Instead of defending and supporting me, he cursed my entire being, the fact that I'd ever been born, the day I was born, and the person who'd given birth to me. My father, whom I'd idolized, whom I honoured and loved, was cursing me because I was weak.

Where could I seek refuge? Where could I escape? Where could I go? If my father felt disdain for me and was willing to look the other way, where could I go?

The second my father looked away and cursed me, I felt utterly alone, so alone. I was like *a nail without a head ...*

My spine snapped at that very moment.

Scorned by my husband, without the support of my father, pregnant with two young children, humiliated and awash in shame … where could I go?

I still wonder, fifty years later, why I didn't leave, why I did nothing.

I couldn't betray my father, although he had just betrayed me. I couldn't subject him to the shame of having a daughter with neither a husband nor a roof over her head. I hadn't been brought up to act like that. Because this father—who'd stooped to insulting the memory of my mother, a woman who'd borne a daughter who'd just let her husband split her lip open—had taught us to respect him, to honour him, to respect our brothers and our husband, and to rely on the support of men. Because this father, and his entire community of men, and women too, had taught us to be submissive, to remain silent, to reveal nothing, to feel ashamed, and to endure everything.

Although we didn't even realize it, our muzzle grew tighter as we grew older … *Bury your despair in your heart and suffer in silence; revealing your misfortune just brings about scandal and disgrace …* All women were shaped by these words, which they murmured quietly to themselves. I was one of those women, and I still am.

Having preached the principles of honour and dignity far and wide, having always protected the weakest and the most destitute, did my father think that his daughter could get by without parental support? Or perhaps he felt that taking care of the poor was preferable to taking care of his daughter's children, who would have been his responsibility if I had deserted my husband. That way, he would be able to avert scandal, keep up appearances, and keep everything hidden so that no one would know anything, and everyone could wash their hands of the matter.

After teaching us to depend on the support of men rather than defending ourselves, they let us fend for ourselves. At the very moment we most need help, they let us grapple with our fate. Was it our destiny to produce men in the image of their fathers and then remain silent? I'd heard so much about honour and dignity since I was a child—were they simply empty words or words invented by men for men alone?

Where could I go?

Where could I go with my children, in the last stages of pregnancy? Even if I'd been able to set aside the respect I believed I owed my father, where could I go in 1945, in a country where wars, big and small, locusts, epidemics, and famines were raging without rhyme or reason.

Where could I go?

Where can a nail without a head go? I am ashamed … I am ashamed … Even though death or resignation were the only alternatives, as I now know, I still feel ashamed to the core and will never forgive myself ….

Every time Abdallah falls ill, I once again see an ashtray, as thick as three plates, crashing against my son's head and splitting open his forehead. The man I'm no longer able to call my husband—because I detest him so much—had hurled the ashtray at his own son. Every time, I once again picture that boot wounding my lip while I did nothing. Every time, my arm breaks again, my heart bursts, and I writhe in pain and loathing because I did nothing that day. I did nothing to defend myself, I did nothing to defend my children. I let it happen to me—I always let it happen.

I am a coward, nothing more than a fearful and cowardly person, a spineless woman without dignity. How can I come to terms with what happened that day, when I couldn't muster up the strength to resist, to make even the slightest movement or gesture, if only to spit in the face of those two men on horseback? Even if the spittle had fallen back on my face … then, at least, I could have told myself today, Dounia, you did what you could.

But no.

I allowed myself to be crushed by pain, my tongue glued to the roof of my mouth, my arms glued to my side. That's all. That's all I did. That's all I was capable of doing. When you resign yourself to something once, you'll be resigned to it for the rest of your life … The damage is done. You can never climb back up. Because one wrong breeds another. And it's endless.

I should have killed him, to rid the world of his violence and depravity, for he wasn't worthy of being the father of my children. I should have killed him with my own two hands to prevent us all from falling prey to his tyranny, to avoid being punched and kicked …

The woman my grandchildren love is not this woman buried under a pile of fat, pain, and shame—she is the child I once was, who sometimes returns to inhabit my body for a few fleeting hours.

How can I tell my daughter that her brother's illness—the one she so desperately wants me to talk about so she, too, can understand—is nothing but bad luck? Because it's her father and his entire lineage who should have been treated, because it's me, her mother, who should have been treated. I'm the one who is completely crazy for having loved a crazy man, for having had children with him, for having let him do whatever he wanted, and for having allowed him to shatter the entire family.

How can I admit that it's my own lack of dignity that destroyed my family, that it's my own weakness and lack of courage that caused our ship to capsize? How can I recount all the violence I was subjected to without reacting, how can I speak about my shame, my resignation, my resentment, my bitterness, my hatred, and my cowardice … without wanting to die … without dying?

How can I tell the truth, when I've hidden it for so long? How can I now say that my own father was a coward and a liar when I've always called him a righteous man? How can I say that, deep in my heart, I have no respect for him? How can I admit that I hate him, without trembling?

How can I say that I've lost all respect for my husband, the father of my children, that I've even hated him at times, and that all I have left is pity because he's old, lonely, and miserable? I can't tell them all of this—he's their father after all. I've always done my utmost to make my children love and respect their father and I can't tell them all that he did ... and all that I didn't do ...

It would be ridiculous to leave him now. I should have made that decision long ago, when my legs were still slim and my body robust, when I was still wearing my wedding dress, which he practically ripped off my body ... But I loved him ... I still love him ...

Today, I wonder who is most to blame. The one who hits or the one who allows herself to be hit, or else the person who watches it happening but doesn't do anything?

Salim is dead. The father of my children is no longer with us. I have wished for him to die so many times and now that he is gone, I feel so alone.

Life is peaceful. There's no one left to contradict me, no one left to bicker with every day, to drink coffee with—coffee that he liked very sweet without cardamom, while I liked my coffee with just a touch of sugar and a grain of cardamom. No one left to complain, grumble, or wish for death when life feels too hard or too monotonous. No one to leave the toilet bowl and bathtub dirty and fill the ashtrays until they overflow. No one to snore at my side and keep me awake at night. Now there's no one to go pick up fresh bread, speak on my behalf, or tell me what he's read in the newspapers, which he's left scattered around. No one to criticize everything I do, to get annoyed when I'm scrubbing the floors too hard. And no one to share in the living hell that we experience, year after year, whenever our eldest son drags us down with him. No one left to hold on to hope either.

My companion in life, suffering, arguments, and laughter is gone. My joy and my pain are gone and buried with the person I both loved and hated so much.

Salim the orphan no longer needs Dounia the orphan. Orphan Salim, who so desperately needed to be loved, no longer needs anything at all.

I had longed for peace and quiet … and all I hear now are the creaking of the rocking chair and hum of the empty fridge.

I wish I could drink a jug of wine to numb this unfamiliar sensation.

I've lost the ramparts that defined who I was. I no longer know where I begin and where I end. I no longer know how to think, or what to think. I no longer know anything. When he died, Salim took away the skin we shared. I'm cold. I'm so cold.

Salim died according to his wishes. Without suffering. Without being restrained in a bed with rails around it. He always said that the day he was no longer able to do everything he wanted to do, he would take his own life. He spoke about it so often that I didn't know whether he would have done it …

On the eve of his death, he told me a story about his earliest years in Canada. The man who'd loved to talk so much, who would tell the same story twenty times over, had waited all this time to share this one with me. If I have the strength, I'll tell Myriam the story when she comes over. Otherwise, I'll soon take it with me to the grave …

At the time, the children and I were still living in Lebanon. Salim had just arrived in Canada and had been living at his mother's home in Sainte-Thérèse for a few months. He wasn't getting along with her. He didn't have any money, and his mother didn't want to help him. He had no trade or work experience because he'd never really held a job. He didn't know the language and had no future. He felt lonely and desperate. One day, he was visiting a cousin who lived in downtown Montreal. He couldn't sleep. Since he had nothing to read, he began to write me a letter of farewell, in which he asked for my forgiveness. He said that he loved me and our children but wasn't able to support us. He said that I'd be better off as a widow than staying with a good-for-nothing. The next day, he left the letter there and set off. He'd decided to end his life by jumping into the river. Since he didn't know how to swim, he thought that would be the best way to die … While walking on the streets of Montreal, heading toward one of the bridges, he came upon a barbershop owned by someone he knew, an old Lebanese man who'd immigrated to Canada in the 1920s, I think. Unlike many others, this man knew how to read and write Arabic, and therefore had books and newspapers in his shop. The old man saw Salim and invited him to come in. For once, Salim had no desire to talk and wanted to keep on going, but the barber was so persuasive that Salim ended up going in. At that moment, a customer came in to get a haircut. Salim wanted to leave, but the barber once again insisted that he stay, saying that he really wanted to talk to him. He handed Salim a book to keep him occupied for a while. Salim liked reading so much that he began to browse through the book. Without realizing it, he read a story that opened his eyes and heart, like the right key in the right lock. He pulled himself together and found the courage to keep on living.

When he finished his story, Salim fell silent for a long time. Then he said, "You never know when a book, a sentence, or even a word can hit you at exactly the right moment and help you change, and continue living … Maybe it would have been better if I had died that day … But, on the other hand, Dounia, you would have missed me. And if not me, then at least our arguments!"

Darling Salim, he could always say something amusing, to make me like him better, to make me forget his bad temper and mood swings.

The man who made me laugh and cry didn't need to take his own life. His heart took care of that. Then death, like the hunter who wrings the neck of a wounded little bird, did the rest. Salim was in his car in front of the house. He was coming home after delivering food to Farid, who was suffering from a mental and physical breakdown that prevented him from working for a while.

After his first heart attack and even after the second, Salim said, "I don't want to die before my time." For him, dying before his time meant having to take care of his health, taking medication. Being careful about your health was for old people. He was not old. He was going to die young. He didn't want to live diminished.

He always said that he wanted to die before me. I would reply with a chuckle, saying that it was out of laziness rather than love for me. He would say, "No, that's not it." But he didn't elaborate.

I now know, since I am living through it, that Salim was afraid of being left alone. He had sensed that living without me would be like entering *terra incognita*. It would be a new form of exile. He didn't want to adjust to anything new again, go into exile again, and feel death creeping toward him. He could feel what it would be like to live alone after spending a lifetime with me, but I'm the one who is actually living like that now, while he is at peace … He always thought of himself first, to the very end … When I mentioned the nursing home to the kids, he didn't say anything, but his silence spoke volumes.

Abdallah has been in the hospital for months, perhaps years. This breakdown was as violent as the first ones he had when he was still a very young man. His mind had already begun to falter a few weeks before his father's death. It exploded, burst into flames, and no medication or shock treatment has been able to extinguish the fire. Reality is intertwined with dreams, and he jumps from one subject to another, from one idea to another, from one life to another without knowing which one he's in.

He calls me often. I listen but I can't cry. I'm tired of everything, even of my own son, who can't come back down to earth anymore. Sometimes, I tell myself that he should stay where he is. It would be better for everyone. What will I do when he leaves the hospital? When he's nothing more than a shell of a man, in a dirty bed, in a dirty room? I don't have the strength to think about it. Salim escaped just in time. I am trying to hold on to hope, alone. But I don't have the strength to hope.

Death hovers over our family. I feel that it's not over yet.

Sometimes, my children and grandchildren visit me. But the few minutes they spend with me are no longer enough to make this gloom dissipate.

Sometimes, she sits in her chair, but most of the time she is in her bed, the wreck of a woman that I have become. She looks out the window, the woman without legs. Her eyes barely see anymore, and she is mute. She speaks to the windowpane in front of her, the woman who has always remained silent. Outside, there's no one. Beside her, there's no one.

Someone comes. A woman dressed in white comes to help her eat. Or else it's a tall, strong man who lifts her into her chair and then puts her back in her bed a few hours later. Sometimes, her children come to see her, acting as if they were doing her a favour, for this woman who has loved them so much. They spend fifteen minutes with her—if that— and then rush off, leaving this woman who has given them everything.

I no longer have the strength or the eyesight to watch television. I wish that someone would sit beside me and tell me stories until I fall asleep.

I have nothing left but these four walls. I told them I wanted to die. They said that it didn't work like that. I said, "I want to die." They removed everything that could kill me. They took away every living thing. When they draw the curtains, it's unbearable. And yet, I can't seem to die.

I've been here for years, perhaps months, or just a few days. When my mind drifts back to the past, it sometimes sees pleasant things. When it looks forward, it sees only the windowpane and grey water beyond. Have I lived my entire life to end up like this—more silent, more alone than I've ever been?

I had legs before. I lived in a house. I came and went. I even invited my children over for meals. I had a balcony where I could sit outside, look at the sky, and watch the passersby, with eyes that could see. That was before.

My life has been turned topsy turvy so many times. I've found myself in total darkness so many times. Then the light would return, and I would quickly come back to life. Oh my God, yes, life! Even here, life is victorious, if even for a few moments. Even here, I surprise myself by thinking of beautiful things that make me smile. Even here, life clings to me and refuses to leave me.

I have lost a lot of weight since coming here. My husband didn't have time to lose weight. Heart disease is a good one to have. The man who comes to move me around twice a day is pleased. My children, too. They say that it's better for my health here. My health! People talk such nonsense.

It's hard to endure silence; it's like a dead weight.

I've lost everything, even what I used to call my wisdom, although I never really believed in it.

All I have left is this bed with rails.

One of the most beautiful deaths was the death of my aunt, my father's sister, who passed away in Argentina. Her children, grandchildren, and great-grandchildren organized a birthday party for her when she turned 106. I don't even know my age anymore. How many years did I stay at home after Salim died? How long did I stay with Myriam, Kaokab, and Samir? How many years do I have left to live before reaching 106? After supper, my aunt danced. After taking a few small steps, she went around and kissed everyone, from the youngest person to the oldest. She could remember all their names without making a mistake. Then she went up to her bedroom. She could still climb the stairs. She fell asleep and never woke up again …

You could not wish for life to gift you a more beautiful death …

I must tell that story to Myriam, I'm sure she would love it.

My children and my grandchildren were here, each one speaking a foreign language. Little Gabriel was grown up. I could understand everything. Salim woke up and said to me gently, "Come, Dounia, let's go to a coffee shop, just you and me."

I opened my eyes and said to him, "I've been waiting a hundred years for this moment, Salim. I've been waiting so long for you to ask me out for a coffee, just the two of us."

He looked at me with a tender smile. I got dressed. Salim was already dressed, but he let me take all the time I needed without saying "hurry up" one single time.

"Take all the time you need, my love," he said, the way people do on television, or the way my cousin Munir used to talk to his wife Karima, whom he adored. And then, out we went, relaxed and chatting as if our whole life was behind us and there was nothing more to chase after. All we had to do was stroll side by side, arm in arm. Salim didn't take the car. Instead, we walked all the way to Wellington Street. The café we chose looked familiar. Salim was smiling and so was I. He ordered a cappuccino and some delicious bread, toasted and served with French cheese, as if he'd guessed what I'd like to eat. He also ordered what he liked—figs and grapes. I thought, "*All his life he had hoped for a single grape, and when he died, he was offered a whole bunch ...,*" but I didn't say anything because Salim doesn't like proverbs. We talked while we ate and sipped our coffee. We looked at each other and sometimes looked out the window, too. We were both calm and at peace.

Salim said to me, "Thanks to you, Dounia, I had a beautiful life. Although my eyes sometimes wandered elsewhere, my heart has always been for you and with you."

I was too moved to answer him. I looked out the window to hide my tears and I saw my children and grandchildren seated at a round table in a coffee shop across the street. They were happy. Abdallah wasn't with them.

"Where is Abdallah? He isn't with his brothers and sisters, Salim. Where is Abdallah?" I asked.

Then Salim turned to me and said, with infinite kindness, "Abdallah is destiny's messenger, sent to teach us something. You must find a way to forgive, Dounia, you have to."

I didn't understand, but I would have all of eternity to understand. We finished drinking our coffee in silence. Then, as slowly as we had come to the café, we started walking back again, at a leisurely pace, as if we had our whole life behind us and there was nothing more to chase after.

It might have been winter or summer, it didn't matter. The weather would have been lovely ...

Glossary

Proverbs or sayings that appear in the novel and inspired the author

فلّاح مكتفي، سلطان مختفي

A self-sufficient peasant is an unsuspecting sultan.

ليت الشباب يعود يوما، فآخبره بما فعل بي المشيب

If my younger self returned one day, I would
like to tell it what old age has done to me.

روحي ع روح ولدي، وروح ولدي ٺالحجر

I would give my soul for the soul of my child,
but the soul of my child is made of stone.

ما بيحن عا لعود الا قشرو

A tree can only feel the tenderness of its own bark.

إيد فاضية إيد وسخة

Empty hands are dirty hands.

زبدة الكلام كلمة

The best speech is a single word.

ساعة البسط ما عمرك تفوّتها اذا جاعت النّفس بآش من كان قوتها
Never let moments of pleasure slip away; it
takes very little to satisfy your body.

الموجوع بيتعلّق باحبال الهوى

A person in pain hangs on to the strings of the wind.

ما بيحك جلدك غير ضفرك

When you are itchy, only your own
fingernails will bring relief.

لله مع الضعيف تيتعجب القوي

Allah is on the side of the weak, to surprise the strong.

الناقص خي الزايد

Scarcity is the twin of abundance.

زوجوا الفقراء بتكثر الشحاذين

If poor people marry one another, beggars will multiply.

كان يسلي الغريب عن أهلو

He could make a foreigner feel so comfortable
he would forget his own country.

كلّو عادة حتى العبادة
Anything can become a habit, even religious devotion.

بالعين ما نشافش بالعقل اندرك

Even if you can't see it with your own
eyes, you can imagine it.

يلّي ما بيسلك فيه الكلام ما بيسلك فيه ضرب السيف

A person who is not affected by words, will
not even be affected by the sword.

صعّبها بتصعب هوّنها بتهون

If you make things difficult, they will be difficult;
if you make them easy, they will become easy.

لله ما بيسكّرها من كلّ الماىل

Allah never closes all doors at once.

كلّ واحد بيزرع حقلو بعقلو

Everyone relies on their own intelligence to plant their orchard.

عوّد الكلب و ما تعوّد بني آدم

Dogs bark whereas humans adapt.

من عاشر القوم أربعين يوم يا بيقعد معهن يا بيرحل عنهن

After forty days, you either behave as they do, or you leave.

إذا حبيبك عسل ما تلحسو كلّو

If your good friends were made of honey,
you wouldn't devour them all at once.

اليّ زوجها معها بتدير القمر بصبعها

A woman who is loved by her husband can even move the moon.

اليّ بدّو يقعد مع العوران بدّو يقعر عينو

If you want to live among the blind, you have
to be prepared to lose an eye yourself.

ما تعلّم ولدك الدّهر بِعلمو

Don't teach your child anything, destiny will take care of that.

ما فيه بحصا إلّا ما بتسند خابية

Everything, even the smallest pebble, has its
purpose and can help to prop up the jug.

طربوش بيّو بعدو معلّق بالتّوتة

Their father's tarboosh was still hanging from the branch of a mulberry tree.

استقبل الإنسان ع قد لبستو و ودّعو ع قد عقلاتو

Greet strangers in keeping with their clothing, but bid
them farewell in keeping with their intelligence.

سكّر بابك وآمن لجارك

Close the door and trust your neighbour.

الرّبى غلب عل الّبى

Raising a child is more critical than nursing one.

بدّو يعرف البيض مين باضو والقُنّ مين عمّرو

He needs to know who laid the egg and
who built the chicken coop.

اليّ خلق علق وليّ مات استراح

Those who are born are entrapped, whereas
those who die are at rest.

المال بِجر المال و القمل بِجر السيبان

Money begets money and lice bring on nits.

ما بيتخبّى الحب و الحَبَل و ركب الجمل

It's impossible to hide when you're in
love, pregnant, or riding a camel.

يوم نار يوم رماد

Fire one day, ashes the next.

واحد وحدو مسمار أقطم

A person alone is a nail without a head.

خليها بالقلب تجرح أحلى متطلع و تفضح

Bury your despair in your heart and suffer in silence; revealing your misfortune just brings about scandal and disgrace.

عاش يتمنّى في عنبه مات جابولو عنقود

All his life he had hoped for a single grape, and
when he died, he was offered a whole bunch.

Works by Abla Farhoud

Theatre

Quand j'étais grande. Solignac: Le bruit des autres, 1994. [First produced in 1983]

> *When I was Grown Up*. Translated by Jill Mac Dougall. *Women & Performance* 9 (1990): 120–143.

Les Filles du 5-10-15¢. Carnières, Belgium: Lansman, 1985.

> *The Girls from the Five and Ten*. Translated by Jill Mac Dougall. In *Plays by Women. An International Anthology. Book 1*, edited by Françoise Kourilsky and Catherine Temerson, 103–159. New York: Ubu Repertory Theater Publications, 1988.

La possession du prince. Montréal: Centre des auteurs dramatiques, 1993.

Jeux de patience, Montréal: VLB éditeur, 1997.

> *Game of Patience*. Translated by Jill Mac Dougall. In *Plays by Women. An International Anthology. Book II*, edited by

Françoise Kourilsky and Catherine Temerso, 37–84. New York: Ubu Repertory Theater Publications, 1994.

Quand le vautour danse. Carnières, Belgium: Lansman, 1997.

Birds of Prey. Translated by Jill Mac Dougall. Montréal: Centre des auteurs dramatiques, 2001.

Maudite machine. Trois-Pistoles: Éditions Trois-Pistoles, 1999.

Les rues de l'alligator. Montréal: VLB éditeur, 2003.

Fiction

Le bonheur a la queue glissante. Montréal: l'Hexagone, 1998.

La felicit scivola tra le dita. Translated by Elettra Bordino Zorzi. Rome: Sinnos Editrice, 2002.

Le sourire de la petite juive. Montréal: VLB éditeur, 2011.

Hutchison Street. Translated by Judith Weisz Woodsworth. Montreal: Linda Leith Publishing, 2018.

Au grand soleil cachez vos villes. Montréal: VLB éditeur, 2017.

Splendide solitude. Montréal: l'Hexagone, 2001.

Le fou d'Omar. Montréal: VLB éditeur, 2005.

Toutes celles que j'étais. Montréal: VLB éditeur, 2015.

Le dernier des snoreaux. Montréal: VLB éditeur, 2019.

Havre-Saint-Pierre. In collaboration with Alecka Farhoud-Dionne. Montréal: VLB éditeur, 2023.

Translator's note: Plays are listed by date of publication, except for *Quand j'étais grande*, Farhoud's first play. In most cases, the plays were written and produced earlier. Published English translations sometimes preceded the print versions of the French original. Translations are listed below the title of the original. *Toutes celles que j'étais*, originally intended as an autobiography, was in fact fictionalized, as Farhoud admitted in a published interview; it is therefore listed along with other works of fiction.

www.ingramcontent.com/pod-product-compliance
Lightning Source LLC
Chambersburg PA
CBHW050348030726
47503CB00008B/2677